'Adultery is often sentimentalised in fiction, but in her ferociously well written second novel Molly McCloskey gives it to us straight    In spite of its lyrical title and exquisite prose, *When Light is L*         of sexual self-delusion. But it also has much that's memorable to say about love – not the affair     the real thing . . . McCloskey writes with shattering insight on loss and the way that it can make us feel tender towards the world' *Guardian*

'Though McCloskey has no shortage of ideas, she also engages the heart: she's particularly good on the contrariness of our desires . . . Fans of Anne Enright will find much to admire and enjoy.' *Daily Mail*

'Masterly' *Irish Examiner*

'McCloskey's prose is lovely and light-filled' *Sunday Express*

'McCloskey describes everything with a luminous exactitude . . . It's entirely beguiling' *Mail on Sunday*

'Luminous . . . As a narrator, Alice is a combination of coolness and intensity, passion and unsentimentality, nostalgia and clear-sightedness' *Irish Times*

'McCloskey has the observational eye of the outsider, able to pinpoint the intricacies and mannerisms of the Irish people and landscape . . . But the writing's the thing. Oh, the writing. McCloskey is the master of the metaphor, the doyenne of the deceptively simple sentence . . . Hers is a wondrous turn of phrase, and yet somehow it makes Alice's life and interiority seem all the more real' *Sunday Business Post*

'*When Light is Like Water* is as gripping as a memoir and as intimate as a poem. Molly McCloskey has written a novel that is both urgent and reflective, a tender and unsentimental exploration of love's dark corners. It is brilliant: her finest book yet.' Anne Enright

'The moving portrait of a young woman adrift through a troubled world and in her own heart. Discovering that the unknowable desires and passions that move her are somehow related to those that drive people to war and conflict, she, and the reader, move closer to a difficult wisdom.' Viet Thanh Nguyen

'Molly McCloskey's prose has such immense authority, precision and seriousness. This shimmering, beautiful, restless work will stir recognitions without seeming to try. If you've ever fallen in love with someone you shouldn't have fallen in love with – as who hasn't, once or twice – be prepared to encounter the novel as mirror, her finest book to date, a triumph.' Joseph O'Connor

'McCloskey writes with such care and craft; every description of the landscape of the west and the life of her captivating narrator is imbued with poetry and truth. *When Light is Like Water* is fresh and raw and completely entrancing.' Sara Baume

'I loved *When Light is Like Water*. It is absorbing, tense, and beautifully written. Molly McCloskey has written a wonderful novel.' Roddy Doyle

'This is a short but powerful novel about love – love for a mother, love for a husband, love for a lover. *When Light is Like Water* will be read for many years to come for its wisdom and precision.' Edmund White

'A powerful and deeply affecting novel . . . In writing that sparkles with intelligence and insight, the ordinary moments of everyday existence are charged with a beauty and tenderness that render them only just bearable' Mary Costello

'Brilliant . . . McCloskey has a limpid, even liquid style: it's as if you were surreptitiously reading someone's chatty and extremely revealing letter' *rte.ie*

'Written with brilliant precision and insight' *Sunday Business Post* Books of the Year

'Powerful . . . *When Light is Like Water* is a tender depiction of love and loss that combines the personal pull of a memoir with the precision of a short story . . . McCloskey's novel is packed with wisdom, and never heavy-handed with it. The details of the affair and the tawdry aspect of forbidden desire are brilliantly related' *Sunday Times*

'A delightful fish-out-of-water account stitched together with gentle yet wondrous prose' *Irish Independent* Books of the Year

ABOUT THE AUTHOR

Molly McCloskey is the acclaimed author of three previous works of fiction, and of a memoir, *Circles around the Sun*. After living for a number of years in Ireland, she now lives in Washington, DC.

# *When Light is Like Water*

## Molly McCloskey

PENGUIN BOOKS

PENGUIN BOOKS

UK | USA | Canada | Ireland | Australia
India | New Zealand | South Africa

Penguin Books is part of the Penguin Random House group of companies
whose addresses can be found at global.penguinrandomhouse.com.

First published by Penguin Ireland 2017
Published in Penguin Books 2018
001

Copyright © Molly McCloskey 2017

Typeset by Jouve (UK), Milton Keynes
Printed in Great Britain by Clays Ltd, St Ives plc

A CIP catalogue record for this book is available from the British Library

ISBN: 978-0-241-97822-1

www.greenpenguin.co.uk

MIX
Paper from
responsible sources
FSC® C018179

Penguin Random House is committed to a
sustainable future for our business, our readers
and our planet. This book is made from Forest
Stewardship Council® certified paper.

'When the dream draws to an end . . . nostalgia
for the impossible will overcome you.'
Jean Thuillier

How do people do it, I used to wonder. Well, I learned. That sort of secret feels like an illness, the way the world slows to a crawl as though for your inspection. So much clarity and consequence – it was like enlightenment, it was like being in the truth, which is a funny thing to say about deceit.

One afternoon at the close of that sweltering summer, when Cauley and I were still in our trance, I found myself travelling west with him by train. I say *I found myself* not to suggest some condition of passivity – I was the one who'd insisted we make the journey – but because when I look back, I have the sense that I'd come suddenly to consciousness right there, on that bockety old orange-and-black train, as it made its clamorous way across the countryside. We were standing between carriages, jostled by the train's motion. A wheaten light streamed through the open window, fresh air was flooding in, too. The day's heat was fading to a sweet residue. We braced ourselves against the wall, drinking bottles of cold beer and sharing a Silk Cut. Those were the days when no one minded if the air was fouled with smoke, the days when you could slide down the window in the door and hang your head out, happy as a dog.

I pressed my lips to Cauley's neck, which was cool and sticky. Cauley was fair, and in the heat his skin got clammy as a baby's. Together we watched the country slide past in frames. The fields, green and empty, or full of sheep who didn't stir when we whooshed by. Then patches of weedy, cracked tarmac surrounded by chain-link fences. Then the back gardens of houses, with their propped bikes and their coal bunkers and the flotsam of family life. And then all was green again, and there were cows where sheep had been, and a breaker's yard, and a bungalow sitting proud on a hill. We leaned out the window and the wind whipped over our faces, and I felt as alive and unencumbered as if we'd hopped a boxcar.

I was married at the time, but not to Cauley.

I found our old house, Eddie's and mine, on the internet not long ago. It's for sale. I track him, on occasion, through the vast electronic undergrowth, imagining who we'd be now if things had gone another way. The first time, I'd only meant to look around the neighbourhood, to get a glimpse of the façade. I wanted to see the mountain, and the view of the Atlantic, the fuchsia that grew at the corner of the drive. But what came up when I searched were the property websites, and there was the house, listed by its name. I'd forgotten it even had a name.

I am doing it again, sitting in the third-floor bedroom of my temporary home in Dublin, clicking from picture to picture, a thin sense of omnipotence upon me. There are things I recognize. A standing lamp, a pair of leather armchairs, the dining table we chose together. Furniture surprises me with its betrayals, its easy migration between lives. What I didn't notice until today is something my mother gave us, the last time she visited. It's hanging on the wall in the spare bedroom, a print she bought in town and had framed – abstract and muted and thus somewhat out of character for her, which was why I had liked it: I couldn't figure out what had drawn her to it. Did I forget to bring it with me when I left? Or did it just seem petty to start taking things off the walls? My mother is dead now, she died eight weeks ago, and I cannot decide how I feel about the fact that some part of her has remained in that house without me.

Also on the wall, taped up in the kitchen, are drawings made by a child, or children. In the living room, a few framed photos that refuse to sharpen into focus. Otherwise, the interiors are oddly impersonal. Eddie remarried several years ago, but the master bedroom has been stripped of anything that might indicate the kind of couple who've been occupying it. It looks unlived in, like a bedroom in a B&B.

Eddie and I bought the house from a woman who suffered from anorexia. The estate agent said she was selling because she was too sick to look after it herself and was going to Dublin, where she had family. She wasn't there on either of the occasions we viewed it, though there was one photo of her on the kitchen windowsill, standing with someone who might have been a brother. Her skin was a strange nut-brown. She wore big, round glasses that made her face look small and childlike, and her neck was like a stick. Eddie said under his breath, 'God love her,' and I slipped my arm around his waist as though to earth us.

The second time we visited, we stood side by side, peering through the big kitchen window which faced the long, western flank of the table mountain that dominated the landscape behind the house. In profile, the mountain looked like a wave frozen at the point of breaking. We were very close to it, on the highest road running parallel, and the large back garden sloped perceptibly upwards. The garden had been let go completely, the growth so thick in places it had thatched itself into a weave. We imagined reclaiming it. We saw a wooden deck, breakfasts al fresco, late nights looking at the stars.

'Shall we do it?' Eddie whispered, and I nodded, rather gravely as I recall. I thought it was what we needed. I thought it would lend our marriage some weight it seemed to lack. We made an offer that afternoon.

After we moved in, I used to go out back on certain summer mornings and hack away at the garden with rudimentary tools. What was wrong with us? We needed a plan, a proper digger and a professional, and there was I with a pair of shears and a rusty shovel and a hangover.

I came to this country at the tail end of the 1980s, when I was twenty-four. I packed up my belongings and stored them in the house my mother shared with her husband in the suburbs of Portland, Oregon, promising I'd be back for them, and intending to be. She saw me off at the airport, both excited and apprehensive. I was her only child, she had raised me on her own, and I sometimes felt her holding my existence in a kind of awe, as though I were newly born. She was also cautious with money, and considered my adventure a little feckless. I was leaving two jobs, one of which she'd been sure was going to lead somewhere. Mornings, I worked at a non-profit that advocated for the homeless and ran a men's shelter, checking people in and out, doing admin or bits of research, sometimes doing not much at all, just hanging around with homeless men in a way that was meant to convey that we – people with homes and people without homes – were all in this together. Nights, I worked in the sports department of a daily newspaper, writing brief summaries of minor games and the very occasional feature. Both jobs tended to muddy the already indistinct view I had of myself. When I was at work in the morning, I imagined I could see a better me on the horizon, someone impassioned and unselfconscious, preoccupied with justice; but at night, surrounded by the buzz of the newsroom, I saw my byline repeating into infinity, growing as big as a billboard, as my fame spread beyond that peripheral city. In other words, I didn't know who I was, or what I really valued, and I began to think that I should take myself away for a spell to find out. I should go to Europe. I had a savings account, into which, each week, I deposited some tiny sum. Eventually, I realized that at the rate I was saving it would be years before I had enough to fund a European tour, and that perhaps I needed to trim my ambitions. And so I went to Ireland.

I flew into London because that way was cheapest, and immediately upon landing boarded the train west for Holyhead and the ferry. I disembarked in Dún Laoghaire on an unremarkable April day, into a hard, white light that surprised me. The breeze was almost balmy, and what looked to me like palm trees along the harbour road added to the illusion that I had arrived somewhere other than an island in the North Atlantic.

I headed north and west, and for two weeks drifted around Donegal, standing on grassy verges, hitching lifts in the drizzle. It was mostly lorry drivers who stopped for me, and I would hoist myself gamely into the passenger seat. From the windows I could see over the hedgerows into the fields. Low walls wormed this way and that, sectioning the land into parcels. The skies were a sudsy grey, or nicotine yellow, or they were charcoal and ready to burst. The drivers all asked the same three questions, and all of them had cousins in New York. They were like no men I had ever met, both knowing and a little slow, faintly lecherous and yet disarmingly innocent. They seemed as awed by me as I was by them, and cast furtive, sidelong glances in my direction, as though I might combust at any moment.

One night, in the fishing village of Killybegs, in a pub down by the harbour, I met a middle-aged couple named Bill and Lil. They were from somewhere outside Derry and for reasons unclear to me kept an apartment in Killybegs. (Was he a fishing magnate? Was it a love nest? Their double act seemed a bit too zesty to pass for marriage.) Overweight and florid-faced, their exuberance tinged with despair, Bill and Lil swept me into their orbit with a desperate generosity. They drank buckets of Black Tower and I drank it with them, over a dinner they treated me to of grilled plaice. At some point I heard myself say – in a manner I'd have thought too unconvincing to elicit any reaction at all, let alone the one it got – that I might go to Galway and look for a summer job. Upon hearing this, Bill heaved himself up from his chair and, with one hand in the air, as though to deliver an oration that would be quoted down the ages, said, 'I know a fella in Galway owns a pub.'

When I didn't protest – there seemed no point; we had entered that state of drunkenness in which life becomes a thought experiment, and we were merely teasing out a scenario that began with my working in a pub in Galway – Bill lumbered off in the direction of the bar, to use the phone.

When he rejoined us he said that he hadn't got hold of this

friend. But he'd phoned another friend. One who had a pub in Sligo.

'*Sligo?*' I said. I hadn't even planned to stop there.

'Who?' Lil asked.

Bill lowered his girth back into the chair. 'Dom Conway. You know Dom.'

'Oh, aye.' Lil looked at me, and her head gave a little wobble of pride. 'Bill knows lads everywhere.'

'You're to call in to him tomorrow.'

'Tomorrow?'

Lil asked if I'd ever done bar work. I looked around. The woman behind the bar was chatting to a guy whose little finger was a stump at the knuckle. She was holding a tap in one hand and a pint glass in the other. The lager ran down the inside of the glass until she knew without looking that the glass was full. She let go of the tap and it slapped back into place, then she flicked a beer mat down like she was dealing a card and placed the pint atop it. There were other people sitting at the bar, all of them men, all with hands like paws. The barwoman chatted to them as one, leaning back against the countertop behind her, her arms crossed. When someone shook a smoke from his pack and offered it to her, she took it and lit it, then left it to smoulder in one of those old glass ashtrays you could brain a burglar with. There were small tables around the lounge area, and maroon-upholstered benches along the wall where the courting couples sat, primly dressed, looking shy and virginal. At intervals, the young men would approach the bar and get a pint for themselves and something mixed for their companions. Everyone regarded everyone else with a strange blend of intimacy and disregard.

'I've done a little,' I lied.

We stayed well past closing time, and although we had long since run out of things to say and kept falling back on talk of my new job and what a brilliant spot Sligo was, I was carried on the wave of their enthusiasm. We raised our glasses a dozen times in triumph. At some point, Lil got out a camera and we took Polaroids of each other. We arranged the prints on our small round table and cooed and clucked as they developed, as though we were viewing a basket of kittens. Then Lil, suddenly serious, gathered up the photos and turned to me, with that dumb and startled look that is the mark of someone drunk and burdened with an emotion that eludes expression, and pressed them into my hand, like ducats for the road, or amulets for my protection.

I checked into a youth hostel in Sligo town that faced on to the river. The proprietor at the time was an openly gay black Frenchman, and this gave me a completely skewed idea of what I should expect from the town. The front room had a large plate-glass window, and in a parallelogram of sunlight that lay across the manky carpet a pair of beautiful Danes played chequers every day, rearranging their long limbs at intervals. When they weren't playing chequers, or out hill-walking, or cooking brown rice, they did nothing, in a way that seemed to me distinctly European. There was one other long-term resident – a willowy young Irish woman named Jane who was a student at the local technical college. Jane talked about 'the environment' and alluded to political corruption as though it were a thing we had discussed at length and were in agreement on. She was canny and sceptical in a way I wasn't used to, and she intimidated me. Every day at five o'clock she tuned the transistor in the kitchen to RTÉ1 for the news on Tiananmen Square. This was often around the time I had to go to work – I had five shifts at Conway's – and in my white blouse and black skirt I would head out past Jane and the Danes, feeling foolish and American.

I had imagined Conway's as the kind of sleepy, familial scene I had witnessed in the pubs in Donegal, but it was frequented by a different kind of crowd – bank clerks, nurses, solicitors and civil servants – and most nights they were three deep at the bar. One weekday evening when it was quiet, I was told I could clock out early. As I headed to the door, two guys I had never seen in the pub before invited me to go elsewhere with them for a drink.

'We'll take you somewhere interesting, somewhere you'll enjoy,' they said, as though they knew exactly what would interest and amuse me, which was not a million miles from the truth. To be a young American woman in a small Irish town in the years when foreigners were still scarce was to enjoy the status of a minor celebrity, and I was growing used to the fact that many people of whose existence I was completely ignorant knew where I worked, slept and ate my lunch.

Their names were Frank and Martin, and they took me to a pub on Bridge Street where the stuffing erupted through vinyl benches and the air stank of patchouli. It was smoky and dark, and the women wore harem pants. We met two friends of Frank and Martin's there. They had all been in a band together, had almost made it big in some hazy past and were, I gathered, ever on the brink of making a comeback. Frank was the drummer, and he had tight curls and a driven intensity that had no obvious outlet. The others were different: pensive and enigmatic. They had lank, rained-on-looking hair and an air of aggrieved entitlement, like people who'd been done out of an inheritance. At closing time, Frank said we were all going out to the beach at Lissadell, and I squeezed into the back of someone's clapped-out Micra and we sped through the dark without seat belts. At Lissadell we sprawled on the sand, and Martin lit a thick, crooked joint that tasted mostly like a cigarette. We passed it among us, and as I stared up at the velvet sky, the heavens seemed to pull up and away, as though they might lift us right off the earth with them.

I met the band guys regularly after that, and soon I was venturing into the edgier pubs on my own. One night in the pub on Bridge Street I met a Canadian woman, about my age, named Camille. She was a stranger in town, too, but far less self-conscious than I was. She was here because she'd met an Irish woman the previous spring in Toronto, and they had fallen madly in love. Camille had followed the woman back here, and they had set up house in a damp cottage a few miles from town. But the woman had, almost immediately upon their arrival, broken it off, and here was Camille, rolling with the novelty of it all and planning her next move. She was stunningly beautiful. She had a pixie haircut, bleached blonde, and was slim as a schoolboy. She wore white V-neck T-shirts and tight jeans and combat boots. When I met her she told me she was planting a garden using the only implements at her disposal — a spoon and a fork. She didn't drink much, but she loved a party and would sit squashed skinnily in our booth, as though she'd been born to this.

When a group of us was out for an evening, there was always a moment when the night either petered out in good sense and an air of anticlimax or assumed a sudden momentum, as though time were running out on something, and it would begin again, that urgent merrymaking with no apparent cause. What Ireland at the end of the eighties often resembled was a place celebrating, insistently, its own collapse, and there was a certain dignity in that, a triumph even.

At closing time, we'd all stumble over to Martin's bedsit, where we smoked sprinklings of hash mixed with tobacco. It burned my throat and left me with a dim, headachey high and a passing sadness for my new friends: this way of getting stoned, so parsimonious and approximate, seemed emblematic of the way they made do. I knew that one day a week they all went to the dole office. I imagined it as one might a methadone clinic or a needle exchange, and I hoped for all of our sakes that I would never see them coming or going from there.

I met Eddie in the midst of those weeks, trailing a hangover that was beginning to feel cumulative. Normally, after a heavy night, I would lie late in my bunk, then trudge about the drab town, past the window displays of cheap shoes and flouncy dresses, past the butchers' shops with their hanging carcasses that sent a smell like sour milk on to the street. I would eat my lunch in one of the teahouses, a toasted cheese or puréed vegetable soup, dutifully reading my paperback Yeats or attempting to work though the thicket of cross-referencing and assumed knowledge that was the *Irish Times*. But the day I met Eddie dawned so fine I roused myself at a reasonable hour and borrowed Jane's bike and pedalled out the sea road to Rosses Point. The gorse was scrambling up the hillsides and the skies were freshly blue. The world gleamed in a wash of wet yellow light. When I got back to the hostel the Danes invited me to join them for an early supper. They made a salad of cucumbers and butterhead lettuce and those tomatoes that tasted of nothing at all, like something astronauts might eat. They'd cooked a fresh fish whole, which the three of us flayed messily and devoured, sitting on the grass in front of the hostel, looking out across the bay to the Atlantic.

Just before six, I put on my blouse and skirt and set off for the brief walk to Conway's. I was in good spirits, I felt clean in my skin, and hopeful, though of nothing in particular. I saw myself as though from above, walking jauntily up O'Connell Street in the lingering sun of early evening, and felt fond and a little nostalgic, as though the night ahead were an experience I was already looking back on.

When I walked through the door of the pub, I saw a man sitting at the end of the bar, chatting to Dom's wife. He followed me with his eyes as I moved behind the counter and began unloading the glass washer. When Dom's wife wandered off he ordered a pint of Guinness, and I served him a thin-headed thing he didn't complain about. I guessed he was in his early thirties, though his hair was already thinning. He had heavy eyelids, which left him looking both sleepy and aroused, and a nose that made me picture his profile on a coin. He was a big man, and he had the look that big men often do – unguarded, somehow made vulnerable by their very heft, like certain slow-moving animals, so that you do not know whether to regard them with pity and tenderness or, on the contrary, to exercise extreme vigilance in their presence. He thumbed through a paper, and when I passed his way again he looked up and held my gaze, and I felt embarrassed by the lowliness of my work. In his crisp, striped, button-down shirt, he appeared to be a man of means. I could see he was like none of the friends I'd made in town.

'So what brings you here?' he asked.

'Vacation,' I said.

'Some vacation, eh?' He looked around.

I smiled. 'What do you do?' It was a very American question, and I immediately regretted it.

He took a big swallow of his pint. It left a line of foam on his lip and he ran the tip of his tongue expertly over it and sat up a little straighter. 'Furniture. I import it and export it.'

I didn't know what to say. I knew nothing about furniture, and even less about importing and exporting. Over his left shoulder, the sun was coming in through the tall windows that faced on to O'Connell Street. It was the summer of a general election and I could see a streetscape quilted with candidates' posters, a confusion of faces buckling on the lamp posts. I wished I knew enough to remark on it all, something pithy and elliptical, the sort of thing Jane might say. But it was an event I couldn't gauge the seriousness of – all the tattered bunting and the megaphones blaring from the roofs of cars gave it the feel of an election in a banana republic or a student council campaign.

'What I meant,' he said, realizing that he'd reduced me to silence, 'was how did you end up *here*.' He tipped his head to indicate Conway's.

'Oh, *here*,' I said, and I told him about Bill and Lil. He listened closely, shaking his head every so often in enjoyment. I smiled again, and tried to look adventurous without giving the impression that I'd do whatever any passer-by suggested.

'So you're around for the summer?'

I hesitated. I didn't want to say that I'd be leaving at summer's end. Nor did I want him to think I was indentured to Conway's indefinitely. I looked down and noticed an after-image of ketchup on my cuff, and said, to my own great surprise, 'I'm thinking of going into journalism.' Was I? Why not? Judging by those campaign cavalcades, the public sphere was slight and unserious, nothing I couldn't get a handle on.

'Really?' He sounded unfazed. That was Eddie, I would learn. I could say almost anything – even things I surprised myself with – and he'd hardly bat an eye, and I never did figure out if he really believed in me, or if he just didn't take my notions too seriously.

'I worked at a paper at home.'

'You were a journalist?'

'Trying.'

He gave me a soft little smile, and said, with the gentlest hint of world-weariness, 'Sure, what more can you do?'

We made a date for the following Sunday.

On the weekends or my evenings off, Eddie would pick me up and we would zoom through the countryside, his Triumph gripping the road, the hedges pressing in with their full summer growth. We went for oysters in Oughterard, and smoked salmon in Westport. He took me to a castle in Kerry and another in Donegal, and to big country houses and tiny little pubs, where in dark nooks we canoodled over milky pints. He took me to an island of beehive huts, to the Shannon, to a bistro the far side of a border checkpoint where helicopters hovered overhead. He took me to an abattoir, and I saw the blood running down the gutters and met a man in spattered coveralls who was charmed by my interest in slaughter.

Sometimes we just drove and drove, to a waterfall or a piece of land he hankered after or a high-up boreen with a particularly fine view. Everywhere cottages crumbled. I had the foreigner's eye – acquisitive, ignorant, romantic – and I would say as we passed, 'What about that one? Do you think that could be fixed up?' and sometimes he would laugh, and sometimes he would weigh the possibilities, and sometimes he would tell me a story about who owned the land and the intractable knot the deeds were in. And I would be astounded that such places should be let go to ruin as though they were nothing, that you could buy a plot with a sea view for less than you'd spend on a car.

I recall a single midnight downpour, parked in Eddie's car above the beach at Rosses Point, the world through the windscreen a rich black smear, as though painted in oils. Otherwise, it was the sort of summer in which every day dawned clear and blue and the seas glittered in the sunlight. The sort of summer whose extreme rarity every person I knew attempted to impress on me, so that a certain unreality attached itself to those months. People flocked to the beaches, looking hazardously pale. The first time Eddie and I went to the beach together I could hardly look at him. I had, by that point, seen him without clothes. We'd had our first, somewhat awkward, sex in the flat where he lived above his showroom and office. But it was still the case that I had seen him naked only in shadowy interiors, and I was surprised that day when he stripped down to his trunks – his *costume*, as he called it – and I saw that he was as pale as all the rest. We were on the wide second strand at Rosses Point. For a moment I averted my eyes, as though out of courtesy, and took in the scene. Dogs romped in the shallow surf and children squealed and families munched on sandwiches they'd packed. The beach lacked, like no beach I had ever visited, any tinge whatsoever of the erotic, and I detected a kind of happiness that was simpler and truer than the vehement bonhomie of night-time.

One evening in mid-August we met friends of Eddie's for dinner in Mullaghmore, on the coast, about twenty minutes north of town. When we arrived at the restaurant the others were already seated, two couples at a picnic table outside, scanning the menus, talking without looking up. An apricot tint hung over the harbour, where tiny fishing boats bobbed, and I marvelled at the fact that anyone would take such toys out into the open sea.

Eddie introduced me. They were all professionals, the wives, too – a doctor, a dentist, a solicitor and an architect – and all around Eddie's age. We sat and ordered drinks and there followed the obligatory exclamations of wonder regarding the weather, and then a discussion resumed that had begun before we got there, which concerned the attempted reform of a byzantine European agricultural policy that had resulted in mountains of excess butter and lakes of milk. I tried to look interested, without looking so interested that someone might ask me what I made of it all, but no one asked and no one offered to explain anything, and I was sure I detected a pleasure in the discussion that was independent of its rather dull particulars. There is nothing like the presence of an outsider to heighten one's enjoyment of being an insider.

By the time the food arrived – plates of mussels and black sole, *boulangère* potatoes, broccoli and carrots – the talk had turned to America. One of the men asked what part I was from. I said Oregon, and one of the women said, 'I was at a conference in Seattle once, it rained for four solid days,' and the others laughed and someone said to me, 'You're at home here, so.'

'So tell us about Oregon.'

'Tell us about America.'

'*Explain* America to us!'

Everyone laughed again. I could tell they wanted me to reveal to them some side of America they hadn't seen before, but I also knew that I was expected to demonstrate a weary cynicism about the place, to mock its excesses and presumptions, and the expectation gave rise to a defensiveness in me. One of the things I loved about Eddie was that he was never cheaply superior or condescending. He liked that I came from the New World. He'd never wanted to live there, but he was a businessman and he regarded my country as fast and sharp and entrepreneurial. When he spoke of America it was with amused, half-baffled admiration – the way you might speak of someone who had no shame but who sometimes, in spite of himself, got it right.

I said something about what a big place America was, and how many different Americas existed, and how difficult it was to say anything conclusive about America, or even about Americans – who were, after all, people from all over the world – and they murmured their agreement but seemed disappointed by the sincerity of my reply, its lack of wit or indirection. After that, they didn't press for my opinions, nor did they ask about my plans, which came as a relief. I had no plans beyond the summer, and still felt, as I did with Jane at the hostel, distressingly short of opinions. What they did want from me was to be assured that I was enjoying myself in their country, as though I were a friend's child they'd been tasked with amusing for the day. I said, 'Yes, of course I am,' and one of the men said, 'What's not to like?' And they all chuckled in a way that suggested there were many things not to like and I would discover them if I stuck around. I laughed along, as though I knew just what they meant. But it was one of those moments when all the conviviality and all the laughter seemed only a cover for what lay beneath: a teeming, tricky, intricately coded world.

An earnest-looking young woman came to collect our plates, and when she departed, carrying the stack in her arms like a pile of laundry, the doctor leaned back against the still-warm wall of the pub, surveyed the scene with a proprietorial eye, and said with exaggerated satisfaction: 'We'll never have to go to the continent again.'

*The continent.* Irish people were always zipping off to the continent, to the South of France or Sicily or Portimão, people who seemed comfortable but not terribly well-to-do, and I was puzzled, even vaguely affronted, by the seeming extravagance of it. But I was careful not to say anything straightforward or wide-eyed – 'How often *do* you go to the continent?' – or ever to appear surprised by anything. I had seen that what gave rise to the greatest derision was the tendency of Americans to be both credulous and easily impressed. Mostly I let Eddie talk for us and relaxed into the atmosphere of enveloping disregard, both unnerved and relieved by my relative invisibility and my looming obsolescence.

Just a few days before, Eddie had told me, quite casually, that he had always hated Conway's pub and had come in that evening only because a friend had said there was a Yank behind the bar and he should have a look. We were in town, walking up Harmony Hill, and I stopped. What I had assumed was a serendipitous encounter had in fact been a sizing-up.

'I see,' I said. 'Like a tip on a horse.'

He looked askance at me and shook his head. He actually looked hurt. 'Not at all,' he said.

I felt disoriented, beset by a suspicion that would from time to time revisit me: that there was more to why things happened here than I was capable of comprehending.

'So am I your date for the summer?' I asked.

'Well,' he said, and traced a finger round my lips, 'it depends on what you want to be.'

I tried to leave him, at the end of that summer. He tried to let me. We were testing ourselves. In September, I went to Greece. I said I might also go to Italy, maybe even France, and that in a few weeks I would come back to Ireland for my things and then I would go home. I had no prospects here, after all. Nor did I have the right to stay indefinitely: even impoverished little nations that haemorrhaged their citizens had immigration controls. Eddie said that he would write. He never felt comfortable writing anything, and the letter he wrote to me while I was in Greece was the only one he wrote during our years together. It came to the American Express office in Athens, where I picked it up, along with two letters from my mother. I read it on the train to Piraeus, over and over, and it may be the thing I recall most vividly about that whole trip. It wasn't that Eddie said anything profound or terribly revealing, it was just the tone of it, the fine simplicity of the style and of the sentiments. The presumption – was I imagining it? – that, after I returned to Ireland, I would not leave. Neither of us had wanted to take responsibility for moving the thing beyond a holiday romance, but here was Eddie, writing so easily about the everyday, as though our story were ongoing rather than ending, and what I wanted more than anything was to dissolve into him, into that presumption. Maybe it should have worried me, that desire for dissolution, but I was not sure how grown-up love was supposed to feel and so I took this desire for its true mark.

I took my unhappiness as an indication, too. In Greece, I was lonely and lethargic. But I was trying to prove something, to myself and to Eddie: that I had not disappeared into him, that I had a life to be getting on with, that I, too, could go to the continent. I had come all this way, after all; surely I should visit Europe proper, the cradle of its civilization. And it *was* amazing, the Parthenon floating above the smog-choked, traffic-clogged city, like memory made solid, like thunder itself resting up there on the hill.

On the island of Crete I stayed in the guest room of a woman who was somewhere between fifty and seventy. She was thick-set, draped in black, warted and whiskered like someone in a fairy tale. She had hardly a word of English, and I, of course, had no Greek. But she treated me with excessive solicitude, as though something terribly unfortunate had befallen me, which, in her eyes, it had: I was alone. (Her own children were in Athens and London; her husband was dead; she lived alone now herself, but she had married, spawned, mourned.) She brought me lunches of hard white cheese and thick-sliced bread, and the sweetest tomatoes. Sometimes there were whole fish on the plate, no larger than my index finger, which she'd arranged in a fan shape. There was always a pool of olive oil. Every meal tasted of the sea and of sun. I felt myself coming to rest in her care. She seemed to know something I didn't; she could read my moods. I had a book in which I actually ticked off the days until I could go back to Eddie, until I could allow him to look after me, and somehow she seemed to know what I wanted, and to want it for me, and I took this wish of hers as a benediction.

I went back to him.

In my absence, the season had turned. The mountains were a charcoal green, rucked in a collar of low clouds, and the fields were marshy and rush-spiked. Those ruins that on long summer evenings, softened by moss-fur and the tumble of wisteria, had had the look of walled gardens, in the gloom were as bereft as tombstones. Weather pressed in off the Atlantic, and you felt buffeted and alive, as though at sea. When the cloud cover broke, the rain-drenched blues and greens glistened silver, and the world was as bright as a mirror and it hurt to look.

I rented a little house in town for forty pounds a week. The floors sloped slightly, and the ceilings were low and also sloped. The sitting room and bedroom were covered in a thin, bristly carpet that was hardly softer than an outdoor mat. To get light I had to ply a wall-mounted grey box with fifty-pence pieces, a situation that struck me as larky and amusing, as did so many other things that winter: the three-bar heater that I carried like a handbag from room to room; the gas Superser which, on those rare occasions when I hit its pair of buttons just right and managed to ignite the thing, could heat the small bedroom to the temperature of hell; the way the walls felt as moist as a cave's. No amount or form of heat would dry that house, and my nose dripped like a dog's in the dusky sitting room. But we can live easily with many things, and minor inconveniences can seem infinitely interesting, if we are young or there is novelty or if we are in love.

Eddie lived by the docks, in the flat above his showroom. He'd been working with furniture since his early twenties, when he'd apprenticed himself to a cabinet-maker in the UK. When he came home he started his own small cabinetry shop, which had grown into the import–export business. He had a couple of high-end craftsmen whose work he sold abroad – Eddie had an aesthete's love of fine things (tailored suits, Italian shoes, good wine, handcrafted furniture) that seemed at odds with his otherwise no-nonsense approach to life – but in the late eighties his mainstay was importing middle-of-the-road stuff for bungalow-dwellers.

The flat wasn't much, a space he'd converted himself, but at night I loved to look out the window and see the lights across the water from the housing estate and, further out, the lights from Rosses Point. In a heavy mist, or with the rain coming down like cold grit and the black water slapping against the quay, I imagined us lovers on the run in some desolate Baltic port.

We hadn't talked much during the summer about our past romances. Eddie could be gregarious, but he was tight-lipped about the big things, like money and love, and I had made the mistake of thinking that because he hadn't said a lot about his past it meant there wasn't a lot to say. It was also true that I didn't want to know, not too much anyway. I'd felt safe with Eddie from early on, partly *because* he was tight-lipped; it made me feel he could hold things – the difficult, messy things – and contain them for the two of us. He didn't probe too deeply about my past, which puzzled me in the beginning, because it didn't feel like disregard. With Eddie, I felt both loved and left alone, my privacies intact, and though the formulation struck me then as miraculous, I later wondered if he hadn't granted me freedoms I was too young and unwise to handle.

Not long after we'd met, he had mentioned a nurse from Clare who'd been working at the hospital in town; but it was only that winter, when we were eating dinner in the flat one night, that he told me they'd almost become engaged a couple of years ago. In the end, she couldn't commit to settling down here.

'She followed her brother to Australia,' he said. 'She was hoping I'd come out at some point, at least try it.'

'Weren't you tempted?'

He shrugged, almost apologetic, as though I would think less of him for having played it safe. 'I had a business here,' he said. 'To pack it all in? I don't know.'

'Did you miss her?' I meant, of course, *Do* you miss her? I was imagining the nurse returning, Eddie gone in an instant. I was picturing her in her starched nurse's uniform, bustling and competent and sexy.

'For a while, I guess, I hoped she'd come back.'

'You did?'

He looked at me, quizzically, then smiled. 'Don't worry,' he said. 'It petered out. I haven't heard anything of her in over a year. I don't even have her address.'

My last relationship had been with a man from the newspaper office in Portland. He was older, maybe forty, attractive in a craggy, intelligent, distracted sort of way. He was a columnist, someone I'd admired from afar before bumping into him – literally, we collided on a street corner – in my neighbourhood one night. When I told him I worked at the homeless shelter, he went on a rant about dubious rezoning proposals aimed at gentrifying my employers out of existence. He wanted me to blow the lid off some scandal I hadn't even known existed.

We dated for a couple of months, during which I cleaved to the idea that our chance encounter was a sign that we were meant to be. But eventually I admitted to myself that he was imperious and impatient. He had little sympathy for hesitation or uncertainty or self-doubt, and if I was anything at twenty-three, it was hesitant and uncertain and full of doubt. I knew that if I were to continue seeing him I would need to toughen up, and I wanted that, I really did. I didn't like swimming in doubt. He wanted it, too. But when I thought of how I might become tough and sure, I felt so inadequate to the task that, instead of growing larger over those months, I retreated.

Some of this I explained to Eddie, who winced as though in pain. He said that I was grand just the way I was, and when

I asked him what he meant, he said, 'You don't have to prove anything to me.'

The night we got engaged, we drank champagne in his flat. I sat on his lap, and he asked, 'How does it feel?' and I said, with mock-gravity and not a little awe, 'I feel quite old and serious.' I thought I was on the threshold of my life.

Just after midnight I phoned my mother with the news. She was both thrilled and saddened. Although she didn't say it, I knew she was thinking that what the marriage meant was that I would live very far away from her for the rest of our lives. But she was a woman of curiosity and enthusiasm, and I could tell she was also excited by the idea that I had gone to an odd little corner of the world and found myself a solid and loving man to marry. She, too, had a solid and loving husband by then – Stan, whom she'd met in her fifties – and it eased my conscience a bit to know she wasn't on her own.

My mother had never lived with my father. She had raised me herself, in a cosy, modest house in a suburb of Portland. She worked as the administrator in the philosophy department at a university in the city, which is how she met my father, a professor of philosophy at a college in Maine who had come to Portland for a semester. My mother was thirty-eight that spring. She'd been engaged some years before, and had broken it off when it became clear that her fiancé expected her to fall in line with whatever life decisions he made – a perfectly common assumption in the late fifties but one that filled my mother with dread. My mother may not have known what she wanted, but she knew what she didn't want.

The day after I got engaged was a Sunday, and we were expected at Eddie's parents' house for lunch. One of his sisters was down from Dublin for the weekend and we were going to announce our engagement. On the way we stopped at Slattery's on High Street for a drink. Eddie knew everyone there – the man who was something big at the pharmaceutical plant, two guys home on leave from the Lebanon, a cluster of plump old ladies who were somehow connected to a family celebrating a boy's First Communion. We nestled into a corner table and ordered pints of Guinness. *We're getting married*, I thought, and it was as though the very air between us was charged with the secret. We were sitting on a cushioned bench. Eddie had one thick thigh crossed over the other, and he was wagging his right foot gently. He was wearing beautiful Italian brogues and talking to the man next to him, laughing at something a little too loudly, and then suddenly he turned to me, rested his hand on my leg and asked softly was I okay.

'You okay there, pet? Can I get you something?'

It was there in the tone. I knew that I was loved as I had never been before. I don't mean that Eddie loved me with remarkable passion or insight. I don't mean that I felt most fully myself with him. I mean that, in the strangest way, I felt forgiven. For as long as I could remember there'd been a vague disquiet in me, as if I lived in the shadow of some humiliation whose particulars I could not recall. Until Eddie, until he absolved me, I hadn't known there was any other way to feel.

The pubs closed at one o'clock on a Sunday, and when the time came for drinking up we were all cast out into the grim white light, a vague, half-sad tipsiness upon us. Eddie drove us back through town, down O'Connell Street, past the tea-house where I'd had my lunches the previous summer, past the draper's and the newsagent's and the tatty shopping arcade whose tiled floor was always lethal with the slick of rain; past the hairdresser's with the sign that read, with no comic intent, *Appointments necessary, if possible*; past the doc-tor's with the shingle hanging over the door that read 'Surgery'.

We crossed the bridge and headed north. On the Donegal road, in the dip between Ballytivnan and the river, were the Travellers' caravans. In summer, they'd had about them something brassy and defiant, but now they seemed forlorn. Two small children tottered, dazed or truculent, in the grass on the wet verge. Strewn around outside the caravans were clothes and pots and pans, generators, and furniture, and the whole tableau, even the children, looked like the aftermath of a natural disaster.

Eddie's mother came from farming stock – her people owned untold acres of good land in Clare. She had all the pragmatism and know-how that come with being reared close to the land, but she had, too, a way of swanning into a room that was almost operatic. She knew her wines and made crème brûlée from scratch. Eddie's father came from a different sort of background – a grubby little cottage near the Roscommon border, a bit of land, a few dairy cows. He had migrated to the town as a young man and worked his way up from shop boy at a building contractors' company to manager, then co-owner, before gradually acquiring a number of properties in the town centre. I wanted to like him, for his audacity and lack of pretence, and because rheumatoid arthritis had confined him to a wheelchair, but I never could, for he was also coarse and demanding, and often dismissive. I gathered that he had once been a strapping man of vigour and rough good looks. Now, he sat in his wheelchair, drinking whiskey and smoking cigarettes, and I dreaded the moments, however brief, when we were left alone together. In his presence, I felt frivolous and insufficient. I would attempt to be of use by fetching him something, and then I would feel ashamed for being able to get up and walk. I am certain he thought mobility was wasted on me. Perhaps he thought it wasted on us all.

He and Eddie's mother lived in a house with gardens front and back, which were tended by an ageing man who had been with them for ever. They also had a woman who was there most days, doing housework, and on Sundays helping to cook the lunches we attended; she was flitting and shadowy, discreet to the point of ghostliness. I had never been in a house where there was 'help'. When I was a child, my mother employed a woman named Lula who came every other week to clean. Her flesh was discernible in rolls beneath the tight, nubby polyester tops she wore, and I remember her as raucous and indiscreet. My mother sometimes sat with her at the small Formica table in our kitchen, talking women's talk, and more than once I saw Lula sobbing (I am tempted to say *blubbering*), running a chubby finger up beneath the lenses of her spectacles, which were always misted and oily-looking.

Eddie had two sisters, both younger. Nessa lived in Toronto, but Celia came down some weekends from Dublin, where she was an accounts manager at a bank. She was married to a man named Gerry, who did something in finance. Celia and Gerry dined at Dublin's only Michelin-starred restaurant and had a home-alarm system that knew exactly where they were and would buzz their beepers if there was trouble. Eddie's mother shook her head and said it sounded *ghastly*, by which she meant their entire existence in that money-grubbing and amoral city, not just the fact that it included beepers.

I had nothing much in common with Celia, but I liked her. Unlike Eddie's parents, she never treated me as though there was some secret to belonging I'd never be let in on. She made me feel it was okay that I didn't know how to make Christmas pudding or elderflower cordial and that I came from nowhere in particular. When Eddie and I announced our engagement that day, all of us in the sitting room after lunch, with a fire roaring and a wet dusk settling outside, it was Celia who declared it brilliant news and jumped up from the sofa to congratulate us.

Eddie's mother looked at us with a frozen smile and said, 'Well, I didn't expect *that*.' There was a beat of silence, then Eddie's father cleared his throat and raised his whiskey in a toast.

From my third-floor window I can see the east and west piers of Dún Laoghaire harbour, curling like the pincers of something risen from the seabed. I can see the ferries from Holyhead hoving into view, a little sleeker now than when I was a passenger, and less redolent of exile and finality. What I can see, in fact, is my own point of entry, the port at which I first arrived more than twenty-five years ago. The coincidence thrills me, though it's hardly astonishing. There are few things on earth smaller than this country.

The house belongs to friends of a friend, a retired couple who are in Canada visiting their son, and will later go to Australia to visit their daughter. It is part of a Victorian terrace, and there is an air of decorum and seemliness about it that is like no house I've ever inhabited. My favourite part of it is the entryway, which smells strongly of the sea. This whole island was once under water, and I like to imagine that this large foyer, with its sideboard and its wall mirror and its umbrella stand, has retained the memory of that. I think of shell middens found on mountaintops. I half expect to find a fish fossil in the floor tiles. When I remarked, with wonder, on the smell – 'How lovely to be this close to the sea!' – the owners of the house expressed puzzlement. They claimed never to have noticed it, and I thought to myself: They have really lost it. But within days of my moving in, that once-overwhelming sea-smell began to fade, so that I found myself sniffing hard when I came in the front door, searching for it, missing it.

I've taken the house for six months, until I decide what to do, where to go. After my mother died, I left Nairobi, where I'd been working for an Irish NGO, and took a consultant's contract and moved back here. Over the years, I had sometimes imagined that I might one day live in Ireland again. But it was not until my mother died that I came back. I was exhausted, by work and by grief, and so far from any person I had ever felt attached to, or anywhere that had ever felt like home. When I thought about where home might be I realized, somewhat to my surprise, that Dublin — where I'd lived for a time after leaving Eddie — seemed the closest approximation.

They've got me writing a year-end report on our work in the world's largest refugee camp — Dadaab, in eastern Kenya. This afternoon I'm meeting the head of our Dublin office, Harry, to discuss it, though it is already clear to me that it won't differ radically from last year's. It's not that nothing happens in Dadaab — there are, after all, almost half a million unhappy people there — it's that many things happen but very little changes. Somalis keep arriving. Today I've been reading through case studies written by field workers, looking for a bit of human interest I might include. There was a Somali woman named Hamdi who set herself on fire outside the office. She had five children, their father had been murdered by men from a rival clan, and Hamdi had become a sex worker in the camp to support her family. If she were caught, she risked being burned alive or otherwise put to death, so it was the grimmest of ironies that she had, at the end of her tether, attempted to call attention to her plight by setting fire to herself and almost dying in the process. Apparently, it worked. After several months, Hamdi and her children were resettled in Germany. We can imagine the possibility of a happy ending. Even so, the tale is simply too grisly to include. What I would like to explore in my report, and what it is certainly not my job to explore, is the question of which is more shocking – barbarity, or the capacity to survive it. When I started in this line of work, brutality shocked me more. Now, survival does. For all the times I've seen people come out the other side of horrors with their sanity seemingly intact, I have never really understood how it is done.

I work at a desk beside the window, watching the weather like it's television. This morning it snowed, lightly. The flakes were blowing about, harum-scarum, and it wasn't entirely clear where they were coming from; apart from a few tufty and benign-looking clouds, the sky was blue. When the flurries eventually stopped, a haze formed, slowly obscuring Sutton and Howth. A darkish band took shape along the horizon, growing gradually lighter and more diffuse as it rose, as though the water's surface was on fire and this was smoke. The haze thickened to the point of obscuring the sea itself. The fire went out. Howth and Sutton sank. I saw in every direction only a grey mass, as solid as a rock face.

My mother asked me once, a little rhetorically, 'Doesn't anything surprise you?'

She meant 'surprise' as in 'astound'. She meant I had no sense of wonder. We were sitting in her living room in a retirement complex in Florida, and she was cooing in amazement as I demonstrated, yet again, how text messaging worked. I wanted us to be able to text each other while I was in Nairobi, and that must've been the fourth time we'd gone over it. Each time, she had shaken her head as though she were witnessing the miracle of flight. I believe that a part of her really was amazed, and I thought maybe she belonged to the last generation capable of astonishment.

'It's pretty exciting,' I said, with more sarcasm than I'd intended.

She looked hurt, and rightly so, and I felt like a bully. Anyway, who was I to scoff? I have no idea how text messaging actually works. And that was when she said it: *Doesn't anything surprise you?*

Later, we walked down the back path and sat in a very gentle April sun and waited for the jitney to bring us to the beach. We shared a small bag of potato chips and discovered we both loved the ones with the little pillows of air in them, and neither of us could quite say why, but the discovery felt extraordinary, as though it were something genuinely important and we could not see why it had taken decades for us to stumble on it. For a moment, she seemed positively girlish, beside herself with delight. I looked at her shyly and had to turn my head away for an instant and gather myself. I think I knew by then. I knew somehow that it wouldn't be long.

Still, her death astonished me. Like nothing ever has.

At some point during my last year in Nairobi, my mother, who had been youthful all her life, even into her eighties – her gait steady, her enthusiasm undiminished, her eyes bright – grew abruptly older. I began to mourn her pre-emptively; the mere thought of her caused my heart to buckle. While she was still healthy I made a decision: that I would go and live near her, or perhaps even with her, during her last years on earth. I would go, I thought, before autumn. And then, the next time I was visiting, she had a small stroke – was it the first? I wasn't even sure – and I began to panic. After that I travelled twice in three months to see her.

When she died, my colleagues thought I would stay in Nairobi. They said, *Don't make any rash decisions*, and *One foot in front of the other*. But her death changed me. When I returned to Nairobi after her funeral, I felt my mother everywhere. I was awash in an indiscriminate tenderness I neither expected nor understood. Everything moved me. Everything – from a bird call, to the green of the grass, to the children playing soccer on the pitch near my home – overwhelmed me with its life. I swung between a lightness of being that bordered on vertigo and a sorrow that made the least movement difficult. In my grief, I felt awakened to the world, and a strange, acute euphoria sometimes stole over me. What I felt, in fact, was perpetually astonished.

Harry said he needs a break from the office, so we're meeting at the Fitzwilliam for coffee. He's already there when I arrive. We order, and he asks me first not about the progress of my report but about my mother. Or, rather, how I'm doing since she died.

I shrug. He nods. I say that grief seems to me a set of contradictions.

'It's like the opposite of vigilance,' I say, 'but the apathy is so keyed up. Everything is heightened, or intensified, and yet I seem to care about it all less than ever.' I find it hard to talk about my mother without becoming overwhelmed, and so I talk about my states of mind. I try to be forensic. I say grief is like a drug, or a dream, like a long, slow panic attack, or like seeing everything, finally, for what it is. Harry tells me his father died three years ago, and that there have been times since when he's felt closer to him than he ever did in life. He says he read a lot about grief in the year or so after, not self-help books but stark meditations on death. Seneca and Montaigne and Roland Barthes.

'What does it mean,' he asks, 'when people say, "She's out of her misery"? Why the present tense? Who's this *she* we're speaking of?'

I smile, wanly.

'I like it,' he says. 'I don't believe there's anything after, but I like that present tense that makes no sense.'

Harry is in his late fifties, dark-haired. One of his legs is impaired. I'm not sure why, perhaps he had polio. He might be just old enough to have contracted it before it was eradicated here. He walks with a stick. There is something thoughtful and contained about him, but also a sprightliness. He laughs readily. He seems like someone who has learned the hard way that the best means of surviving it all is a sense of humour.

Harry had wanted to be a historian, but he abandoned his Ph.D. He decided, after seeing a programme on the BBC about waves of displacement during the Angolan civil war, that he didn't want an ivory-tower life. He apprenticed himself to a small NGO and learned everything he could about shelter. He says we met once before, when we were both working for the UN in Kosovo, though I have no memory of it. I thought I knew him only through email, and as a voice emanating from a starfish-shaped box splayed on a table in a conference room. But he insists we were once on the same assessment to a Roma camp outside Mitrovica.

I ask him if he isn't confusing me with someone else, and he keeps saying, 'I can't believe you don't remember.'

'Sorry,' I say.

I'm surprised I don't remember, partly because Harry feels familiar to me, uncannily so, but also because I remember the mission itself, or at least the mood that hung over it. It was summer. It had rained all morning, heavily, and the air was hot and wet. The sky was still low, and a gulley of grey water ran down the muddy slope that separated the shacks. The camp was near a disused mine, and there was a slag heap visible above the tree line. Children gathered around us, listless and blank-eyed. The atmosphere could hardly have been bleaker.

Harry says he read the report I circulated afterwards, and that it was thorough and detailed. The report, I have no recollection of. From my years in the field, I remember little of all the facts and figures and timelines I assembled, assessed, disseminated. What I remember are impressions, and images, and people who were more interesting as symbols than as individuals. I remember Irish women getting deep-tissue massage and complaining about the help, half in love with the ironies of neo-colonialism. I remember the night a Scottish woman – she'd worked in all the world's dodgiest places, Colombia and Iraq and Somalia – stepped out of a bar in Mombasa and was killed by a passing car driven by a drunk German. I remember buying roasted chestnuts from a cart in a square in Belgrade one late-October afternoon when you could feel the season turning, winter setting in smoky and cold, and all around me old, old Europe, so burdened and war-weary and rich in loss. And one evening in Batticaloa that I remember more clearly than any other. I was sitting with three colleagues and two local teenagers drinking tea in a cement-floored room open to the warm night, rubber prostheses – arms and below-the-knees and whole legs – dangling around the room's perimeter like a dozen disassembled mannequins, something vaguely fetishistic about them, when into our midst wandered a big-bellied water monitor, its skin like an oyster shell, looking as old as time itself, and we all went still while, above us, the limbs swayed slightly in the breeze and the five-foot-long lizard oozed across the floor, and though I saw it all for the cheaply surrealist snapshot that it was, I knew that I had witnessed few moments in the world as strangely beautiful as this one.

Sri Lanka had been my first overseas posting, in 1996. I had left Eddie, I'd left our house on the slope of the mountain and fled to Dublin, where I got a job at an architectural trade magazine. One evening I went for drinks with a workmate and her sister, who was home on leave from her job as a protection officer for the UN in Colombo. I had never met anyone who did that sort of work, and I was fascinated. I badgered her with questions. When she asked about my life, I said I was 'in transition', bored to tears with my job and wondering what the next step should be. Before the night was out, she was promising to arrange a phone interview for a volunteer post in the information department of the country office in Batticaloa.

I thought it would be a brief interlude, an adventure. But that sort of life can become a habit. It has a way of filling in the blanks. The *esprit de corps* and the gallows humour and, sometimes, history happening before your eyes: these things tell you that you matter, that your days have a purpose. A form of institutionalization sets in, so that now I have the strange feeling I've been released back into the wild. *Life on earth*, Harry calls it. Meaning a middle-class existence in a developed country where one has no special status and where nothing too obviously atrocious is going on.

'It's a bit of a change,' he says. His tone is wry. Then he looks me in the eye and says kindly, 'Be careful not to isolate.'

'I know,' I say, though I also know that isolating is precisely my impulse when in the thick of grief.

Neither of us moves. We've been sitting for almost an hour and have agreed on an outline for my report. The usual sections: shelter, food, health, sanitation. A special section on camp prostitution, another on security issues and, to show it isn't all doom and gloom, a third on entrepreneurship within the camp. Mostly, though, we've talked about things other than the report. Parents, and mourning. How I went abroad to begin with and where I might settle now.

The changes Dublin has undergone. We are like any two people who have spent a long time in the same line of work. A lot goes without saying, and my report won't reinvent the wheel. Harry looks at his watch, and I look at mine.

'You'll be all right?' He gives me a little smile, so his worry doesn't worry me, I guess.

'Of course,' I say.

'We'll meet next week?'

'Next week?'

'Lunch,' he says happily.

I know what he's doing. He thinks I need keeping an eye on.

'You don't have to,' I say.

'I know I don't.'

For a moment, I have to look away. In my current state, kindness slays me. When I've pulled myself together, I say, 'Whatever day suits you.'

We agree on Friday. Then he pays for our coffees and we step out on to Stephen's Green and say goodbye.

During the year between our engagement and the wedding, I had flashes of doubt about what we were doing, which I felt guilty for harbouring and didn't mention to Eddie. I was in love with him, and wanted badly to rise to the occasion of his offer of his life and his love, but there were things about him that I needed to come to terms with – or not – on my own. I needed to accept that I was leaving my country for ever, because it seemed unlikely that Eddie would ever leave his. I also needed to accept that Eddie was never going to be a man who spoke easily, if at all, of his inner world; that he was a man of doing, not dwelling upon, and that though this might at times inspire a certain confidence – the proof of his love visible in his actions – it might also mean that there was a limit on how deeply I could ever know him, and I felt a stab of loneliness when I thought of this. I felt it keenly not long after our engagement. His mother's oldest and dearest friend had died, a woman Eddie had known since childhood and for whom he'd had great affection. I had gone with him to the funeral, and afterwards to the gathering at her daughter's house, and I had watched Eddie and hadn't known whether to be impressed or disconcerted by his self-possession. The following day I had tried to talk to him about this woman and what she'd meant to him, and I could feel him closing up, shrugging off my attempt. I said it seemed important to talk about these losses, and he said that sometimes silence was a form of respect. I told him that I understood that – but actually I didn't. I thought it was fear, a refusal to allow himself to feel uncomfortable, to lose control even for an instant, and I couldn't help resenting it, that refusal that seemed somehow directed at me – or at life. And yet I knew that he had ferried his mother back and forth to visit this woman in the hospital, that he had visited her himself throughout her illness, and offered practical help to her daughter. I knew that he'd been solid and present, and that, when his mother became disoriented with grief, he had steadied her. But still he wouldn't speak about it all, and I wasn't sure I could live with such silences.

And then, one night, I had what felt like a conversion experience. I allowed myself to accept, with what seemed my whole heart, a future with Eddie. It wasn't a decision (even 'allowed' isn't the right word), and that was why it felt like something I could trust.

It was a spring evening, and I had returned to town from a particularly unpleasant encounter with a man I was interviewing near Donegal town. I had been freelancing for two papers in Dublin, and I occasionally wrote pieces for the horrendous local weekly. The work gave me some sense of having a life – a self – that existed outside Eddie's orbit, though it was piecemeal enough, and my subjects sufficiently trivial, that it also left me feeling more like a Sunday painter than a journalist. The man I met that day had been accused by neighbours of building on land that wasn't his own, and the episode had escalated into news because the man had grown belligerent and begun obstructing a nearby access road with his tractors, and was now receiving anonymous threats to both his property and his person. The whole thing struck me as silly, and I suspect my attitude betrayed this, because we weren't talking three minutes when the man, who was sitting on a bench in a café with his head thrust towards me and his two hands planted on his spread-open thighs, began haranguing me, to the point where I eventually left the interview shaking, ashamed of myself for letting him reduce me to such a state. Heading home in a downpour, I narrowly avoided ploughing into the back of another car as I rounded a bend on the main Donegal road. It had only one dim tail light and was travelling at a crawl in a 100kph zone. I swerved to avoid it and fishtailed on the wet road before regaining control.

The minute I walked through the door of his flat, Eddie could see that I was upset. He sat me down and made me a drink, and I told him first about the near-miss on the road, and then about the Donegal man. He put his arm around me and smoothed my hair. It was pitch black out and I could hear the rain drumming on the windows. I kept replaying in my mind the scene on the road, feeling the car lurching beneath me, the terrifying realization that I was not in control. I buried my face in Eddie's neck, feeling as safe as I could ever recall having felt, and pressed closer to him on the sofa. His hand tensed on my skull, and the moment turned abruptly sexual, and we wound up making love on the floor.

It was afterwards, as we lay there, tangled in our own clothes and still lazily aroused by that unexpected onrush of desire, that I surrendered to our future. Yes, I thought, we can make a life together.

*

We married in Sligo Cathedral on a fresh September day. The reception was at the family home, in a marquee set up on the lawn. The sun shone and a jazz quartet played, and even Eddie's father seemed cheerful. Camille and Jane were my bridesmaids. Two weeks before the wedding, they had insisted on a night out. Jane, who had graduated from the local tech with a degree in environmental science and now had a job monitoring water quality, rounded up three other women, extras whose names I hardly knew, and we went out on the town. None of us was the hen-party type and none of us, at least that we admitted, regarded marriage as a deliverance from the perilous state of being unmarried. But I went along with it, out of what felt like superstition. Camille had gotten herself a job in a Celtic jewellery shop in town and the women had bought me a pendant with one of those triple swirls, which I wore all night and never again. At 2 a.m. they walked me down to Eddie's flat, all of us arm in arm and in an out-of-season singsong of – I'm embarrassed to say – 'Fairytale of New York'. When we got to Eddie's we shouted up to his window until, finally, the sash was raised and Eddie leaned out, like an imprisoned princess, which caused my companions to howl lewdly but reduced me to a besotted silence. He came down and unlocked the door. 'You survived,' he said, smiling sleepily, and I wrapped my arms around him and felt delivered, like a baby, into his care.

My mother travelled over from Portland with Stan. She took to Eddie immediately, which was both a relief and a surprise. My mother had disapproved of every boyfriend I'd ever had, up to and including the impatient columnist. She feared that I would fall for a man of inconstant character and find myself disappointed, and saddled with a future I hadn't bargained for. By then I knew that that wasn't quite how she saw her story with my father, or the task of raising me, but I also knew that her apprehensiveness about my choices was informed by her own life.

She and my father had dated during the semester he was in Portland, a romance that hadn't evolved into something serious. 'We wouldn't have made each other happy,' my mother said, when I was old enough to press for details. When my mother became pregnant towards the end of that spring – a surprise to both of them – she didn't try to persuade my father to stay in Portland, nor did she ask him to take her to Maine with him. It was brave of her, really, to go it alone, but my mother was in some respects ahead of her time. They said their goodbyes and went their very separate ways. At some point during my childhood I became aware that he sent a sum of money every month towards my care.

I didn't meet my father until I was eleven years old. He had sent a letter to my mother, asking her to share it with me if she thought it best. He'd got married a couple years previously. He and his wife did not plan to have children. His wife, however, had known about me since they'd met, and it was at her behest – rightly, he said, for the lack of contact with his daughter had sat uneasily with him for years – that he was writing. He said that he didn't know if he knew how to be a father, or to what extent my mother, or I, wanted him to be. The last thing *he* wanted, he said, was to upset our domestic harmony. He used that phrase – *domestic harmony*;

his tone throughout, in fact, was of such formality that I imagined him ashen and bespectacled, standing at a lectern. He didn't sound like much fun, which didn't mean I wasn't breathless with excitement at the thought of him. I hoped that I would learn something about him that would enable me to understand his capacity to absent himself as he had, something that would cast him in a noble light and relieve me of the suspicion that some deficiency of mine had made it easy, or necessary, for him to stay away. And so began our tentative and, as it turned out, short-lived relationship, an exchange of letters that led to his visiting Portland, on his own, a few months later.

We did well, I think, that weekend, for two people so stunned by the sudden, unfamiliar reality of the other. He was staying at a nearby hotel, and on the Saturday he picked me up at our house and we went for lunch down on the waterfront and took a boat tour up the river. On the Sunday we went to Multnomah Falls for a gentle hike, which offered a context for togetherness without the necessity of constant conversation. In the evenings we had dinner with my mother, which presented its own strain but at least relieved us of the intensity of being alone together. My parents didn't seem overly uncomfortable with each other, and I imagined – what child wouldn't, in such a situation? – what a perfectly nice family the three of us might someday make.

All that weekend there was a palpable restraint in my father, which I decided was due to nothing more than our newness to each other and which I quickly made it my life's great cause to overcome. (The minute he left I wrote him a letter, and I can still recall its effusiveness, a kind of courage I can't but admire.) This project of mine filled me with hope, a hope suffused, as perhaps all hope is, with anxiety, for I believed that somewhere in my repertoire of being existed the equivalent of a magic word – a fact about me as yet unknown to him, a side of me he hadn't seen, the sheer hidden wonder of me – and that I must locate it, so that with it I could perforate that reserve of his, enabling his love for me to break helplessly through.

Oh, what power absence wields. I would've tied myself in knots for him if only I'd known how, and my poor, devoted mother witness to it all. Of all the boys I would pine for in the years to come, I don't think anything compared with the near-slavishness of my desire for my father's affection.

I saw him again a few months after the first visit. He had attended a conference in Seattle, then driven down to spend a day and an evening with us. It was during that weekend that it was agreed I would visit him and his wife during the upcoming summer vacation. This visit never happened, for three months later my father was diagnosed with pancreatic cancer.

I had the feeling my mother was angry with him for becoming ill, which hardly made sense. Later I wondered if she'd suspected him of knowing all along that he was ill and that being the reason he'd finally sought me out – which wouldn't have been the worst crime, and possibly not a crime at all. But I don't think he did know when he wrote that first letter, or on either of the visits. He didn't seem at all sickly and, though he was self-contained, he was nothing like the greying, sedentary figure I'd imagined. He was someone who loved to swim and hike almost as much he loved to read and write, and I don't recall there having been any whiff of morbidity about him.

I was devastated by his death – he was a future snatched from me just as I had glimpsed it – but there was, at the same time, a discomfiting sense in which death seemed to return him to his natural state, for in the years before I met him my father had often seemed oddly posthumous to me, a distant ancestor rather than the person who begot me. I don't know what would've become of us had he lived. I think that, in his own reluctant way, he wanted to know me, and for me to know him. But I think there were limits, too, to his capacity to absorb me into his life, and I can imagine that as I got older and felt the need of a father less, I might've closed the door, unwilling to forgive him his years of absence.

My mother remained single while I was growing up, though she went on the occasional date – perhaps more dates than I was aware of. Her social world consisted mainly of women she played bridge with at a club in Portland and with whom she went to dinner or the movies. From her work at the university, she had developed an interest in philosophy, and sometimes she went to talks on campus and read books that professors in the department had written or contributed to. She was able to immerse herself in some of those books, and she would read out bits to me, wonderstruck; others, I could tell, were too dense or challenging. She would be sitting in her armchair, and a look of self-consciousness would come over her, and she would leaf ahead – to see if it got easier – and then quietly put the book aside and take up something else. My mother was by no means unintelligent, but I have a sense of her as someone caught between worlds, or eras, not drawn to the more obvious and conventional roles available to her but not sure enough of herself to carve out a life of greater challenge or stimulation. She had earned her undergraduate degree in English, and I know that she lived with a diffident desire to be more than a glorified secretary, but being around all those clever men – the department was staffed entirely by men throughout her time there – reinforced her sense of being not clever enough, for though they were all fond of her and relied on her enormously, not one of them encouraged her to expand her horizons, and my mother was someone who needed that sort of permission.

Once, I saw her with a man I didn't know. I was ten years old. I had come downtown with a friend and her older sister. It was the lunch hour of a summer's day, a workday for my mother. We were passing a little eatery, looking idly in the window, and there she was; I could see her through the glass, shaking her head and smiling, as a balding, not bad-looking man gestured rather wildly, in a manner clearly meant to amuse her. Before I'd even thought what I was doing, or considered the advantages of spying on her, I had left my friend and her sister on the street and burst in upon them.

In the egoism of early adolescence, I hadn't seriously considered the idea that my mother might have, or want, or be entitled to, a 'private life'. It was only on seeing her that day – seeing her face when she caught sight of me over her companion's shoulder, the brief, slight slackening of her features as her laughter subsided, that strange look in her eyes, as though she was trying to place me, before she recovered her wits and perked up and said, with what sounded like genuine pleasure, 'Alice! What are you doing here?' – that it dawned on me that I was not everything in the world to her.

She introduced the man as 'my friend David', a professor of English at the university, and he greeted me by way of a courtly nod, followed by a broad smile and an offer to join them. He seemed jovial and hearty and, somehow, not a man I could imagine my mother loving. Anyway, I don't think there was anything significant between her and David, but that isn't the point. The point is that I'd awakened to her loneliness, her sense of incompleteness – which was, after all, perfectly natural – and instead of growing empathetic I took it personally. I made a show that evening at home of trying to convey my upset, while trying at the same time to make it look to her that I was, for her sake, covering up how truly upset I was. I'd like to think she saw through this act, and that those years she went without intimacy were the result of not meeting the right man and not of the success of my manipulations.

What I feared, I think, was my mother erring and the result being a reprise of our first abandonment, only this time – somehow – I would lose her, too. I had one certain parent and one missing parent, and I was not about to gamble what I had in hope of doubling my luck. Meanwhile, I wanted my real father. Throughout my childhood, and even more intensely once I'd met him, I felt my father's absence like an undertow, a pull in the direction of the unknown and the ideal. I imagined that if I transformed into the magic thing – a boy? a girl-child who needed nothing and provided unalloyed delight? – then all the pieces, and the people, would fall into place. Even when I grew old enough to accept that the person I longed for simply did not exist – firstly because my father was incapable of being what I needed him to be, and then because he'd died – the pull did not subside. By then, the longing had detached itself from its object and become something free-floating, something quietly ravenous.

A few nights before the wedding, my mother and Stan and Eddie and I were having dinner at a converted castle south of Sligo. Eddie was talking – about his business and about furniture – and Stan, who had spent most of his working life as a financial planner, was nodding earnestly, saying, 'You bet' and 'You're on to something there.' I noticed my mother looking at Eddie in a very particular way, and I knew immediately what she was seeing: completion, stability, containment. I turned to Eddie. I hadn't really been listening to what he was saying – something about educating people to become more sophisticated consumers – and I put my hand on his thigh under the table. I saw the corner of his mouth twitch. I wanted to run my hands all over him, his shoulders, his broad back, to cup the nape of his neck in my palm. I wanted to consume him. When I glanced back at my mother, I saw that she was looking at me. She gave me a little smile, proud and collusive and relieved. I was safe. Her work here was done.

\*

Eddie and I rented a house in town and commenced being married. It was a small place, and we viewed it as temporary. We had talked about where we might buy a house – whether we could get something near the sea, or maybe in the countryside – but for now I liked being in the town, able to step outside the door and be in the midst of things.

That first year, I didn't feel terribly different, and I wasn't sure if that was an indication that marriage was our natural state or if it meant that some part of me didn't quite believe what we had done. I had the sense that we were still in the prelude of our life together, and I wondered whether this feeling was common to couples who had not yet had children.

Eddie's mother mellowed towards me after we were married, and a certain deference entered her attitude. By assuming the status of wife, I had become, in her eyes, a woman to be taken seriously. This struck me as silly, and the truth was that I felt diminished by my new status. I hadn't changed my name, but when a card or letter came addressed to us both it was often the case that I now had neither a first nor a last name. I had simply been collapsed into a *Mrs*. What disturbed me more than the thing itself, though, was the seductiveness of that collapse. Here it was, a ready-made role that I had only to inhabit, where the expectations were clear and the rewards understood. It was all so simple, or could be if I let it. I felt the lure most keenly on Sundays, when we went to Eddie's parents' place for lunch. There was the proper glass for every drink course – the aperitif, the red and white wines, the liqueur, the port – and as I sat there with a crystal tumbler heavy in my hand, I felt the world acquire a density and depth that it had never had before. I realized that all my life I had felt insufficiently anchored. I recall a certain windswept Sunday — we had all retired to the sitting room for a smoke and a cognac after lunch, the fire crackling demurely in its grate — and feeling a sudden surge of impatience to bring children into this mix, to see them (two, maybe three?) sitting on the carpet like little angels, playing with their wooden toys, and thinking that if I could just give myself to this, this sweet tableau I saw before me, I would always know who I was and who I belonged to and what was required of me.

Our social life revolved mostly around Eddie's friends, the couples he'd introduced me to that first summer, people who wanted nothing from me other than that I enter into the spirit of the evening, keep up with the drinking and occasionally utter something unexpected. They hardly knew me, nor I them, and in their company I found it possible to hide in plain sight.

I kept freelancing for papers in Dublin, but there was only so much news from Sligo that the national media were interested in, and if there was anything really big they sent their own people to cover it. When the regional radio station opened I began to do the occasional story for them: the oldest woman in the county celebrates her birthday; a young man punches a punching bag for a world-record forty-two hours; the efforts of the Tidy Towns committee. My assignments were not enough to occupy me fully, and there were evenings when I found myself exaggerating the labours of the day. Eddie didn't seem to notice, or perhaps thought it normal that I, his wife, should pass hours each week engaged in nothing in particular.

Every so often, I did get to go to Dublin for work, each time boarding the train with a frisson of excitement, and each time feeling more daunted upon arriving. One fine autumn afternoon I sat in the garden of an advertising firm in Ballsbridge with a man named Niall, eating salmon and glass noodles, in a near-paralysis of inadequacy. I was researching a local-boy-made-good piece. Niall hailed from a south Sligo backwater and had gone abroad in the early eighties when the country was economically stagnant and choking on coal smoke. Now he'd come home, all spit and polish, proud to be Irish and with a vague air of plunder about him. Niall embodied an attitude that would become widespread, one that saw the sudden upsurge in the nation's fortunes as a form of moral restitution. He wore pressed denims and slip-on loafers of the softest leather, and a sky-blue cashmere V-neck that set off the traces of grey at his temples. He was demurely wealthy, smooth as agate, and he was giving me an hour of his time. Around us in the garden young people sat on the edge of their cast-iron seats, jabbering excitedly into one another's faces, lit by some creative or acquisitive fire. Gone was the gormlessness I had long associated with Irish twenty-somethings, the slouch, the in-turned shoulders, the physique somehow thinnish and doughy at the same time; gone was that air of expecting, at any moment, to be embarrassed. They looked amoral and eternally young. It was like witnessing the advent of a new species.

Am I exaggerating? Possibly. But I'd grown countrified. I, who had once felt so brash and New World, now felt slow-witted and gauche. Returning home on the train that evening, the clouds gathering over Leitrim, as they invariably did, I could feel my insides tightening, a morning-after despair gnawing at me, as though I had lost something dear to me but could not quite recall what it was.

As the economy improved, Eddie's business steadily expanded. He was well positioned to supply the new housing estates that were beginning to proliferate, and to meet the more rarefied needs of the first wave of nouveau riche. He started to travel more, often just to Dublin but sometimes to England or the continent. In the beginning, I often went with him but, increasingly, I stayed at home. I spent the evenings he was away reading or watching videos or going out with Camille or Jane, sometimes to the little cinema on Wine Street, sometimes for drinks or a meal. One night at closing time Jane and I ran into the guys from the band I'd partied with that first summer and had hardly seen since. Jane was ready to go home, but I agreed to go on with them for a late drink. We went to the hotel on the bridge, a flat-roofed affair from the sixties that must've been the height of luxury in its day but now looked dismal and tired. We got a table in the corner of the bar and ordered pints. I bought a pack of Silk Cut, though I rarely smoked then, and we all puffed away like mad, and the boys teased me about being let out for the night.

'You're made up now,' one of them said. It wasn't the first

time I'd heard that line, or variations on it, and I always ignored it, but tonight, because I was drunk, I said, 'If I'd been looking to get *made up*, this town wouldn't have been my first stop.'

The sharpness of my tone surprised them. Martin tapped a cigarette on the outside of the box. 'Ah, now,' he said.

It was one of those catch-all phrases of placation that drove me insane. 'Ah now, what?' I said.

Frank stared at his lap. One of the others winked at me, not in a smarmy way, but conciliatory. Now I felt ashamed. They had thought of me, in the long ago, as one of them. And all they wanted now was for me to agree that I *was* made up, that we – those of us who cared about things other than money – had got one over on the mercantile class. Only I didn't feel that way. I was an American from the suburbs, and though Eddie's family might've been more polished in some ways than my own, I could hardly view them as a class enemy.

At one point I looked over towards the bar. The man who owned the hotel was standing there – he knew Eddie from the Chamber of Commerce – and he saw me and nodded. His eyes took in my companions, and he hesitated for a moment, then turned away. When I went up to the bar shortly after to order another round, he materialized beside me and said, 'What have you done with himself?'

'Sent him packing,' I said flatly. I was tired of existing only in relation to Eddie. 'He's in France.'

With an oily little smile, he said, 'If it was me, I'd have taken you along.'

'Would you?' I said.

'I would,' he said.

'Well, I didn't want to go. I had things to do here.'

He glanced in the direction of the boys.

The barman said he'd drop the drinks down, and I gathered up my change and pocketed it.

The owner and I looked at each other, the way you do, and he said, 'I should buy you a drink later,' and I said, '*Should* you?' and laughed brazenly and turned away.

The boys and I stayed at the hotel until they stopped serving, and then we went to one of the grungier late-night discos. I danced until two in the morning, and every second person said to me, 'Where's Eddie?'

When Eddie got home the following day I felt unwholesome, as though I had actually cheated on him. He didn't ask what I'd done the night before. He wanted to tell me about the deal he'd closed to become the rep for a line of French dining suites. He was standing in the kitchen, and I came up and put my arms around his waist and ran them up his chest and down again. He squirmed a little, slipped out of my embrace, and said, 'What shall we do about dinner?'

Late that night, as Eddie slept beside me, I was awoken by the sound of a man wailing. It was so tortured and insistent I got out of bed and opened the sitting-room window and poked my head out. He was standing at the corner of Castle Street, wearing an anorak that was hanging off one shoulder. There was another man with him – they looked to be in their late twenties or early thirties – and he was tugging at his friend's jacket, then trying to bear-hug him into submission, like one boxer clinching another. They staggered a little together, and then the howling resumed. Against the wall was a heap of black rubbish bags awaiting collection, and he began to kick at them, while the second man stood there, his hands on his hips and looking down the street, like someone waiting for a dog to do its business. One of the bags burst and its innards spilled on to the footpath. But he kept kicking, and then another one split and caught on the toe of his shoe. I think the indignity of that set him off again, for he became even more tormented. Finally, violently, he shook his foot free, and then he stumbled up Market Street and into the night, his friend trailing defeatedly behind.

I was awed by the man's anguish, or rather by the force of its expression, and I had trouble getting back to sleep. When I described the scene to Eddie in the morning, he shook his head with bemused, absent-minded interest, the way he did when I told him a dream I'd had. 'I wonder what happened to him,' I said, and Eddie said, 'He was rat-arsed, that's what.' Then he kissed my cheek and headed off to work.

I was unsettled in the weeks that followed. I felt itchy, and nearly petulant with boredom. Eddie's ease irked me. A resentment had surfaced in me after that night out, which had something to do with my life having been decided and defined, with the admission that I had not entirely submitted to that finality, and with the fact that Eddie didn't see this, or couldn't see it.

*You're made up now*, I heard the boys say.

I thought of the hotel owner, his eyes on me, his proprietorial tone. My being Eddie's wife somehow gave him the permission to speak to me like that. I felt repulsed by it. I also felt a shiver of desire.

One afternoon, coming home from doing the shopping, with a bag of groceries in each hand, I was passing by the open door of a pub on Wine Street, one of those dark unsavoury spots I had frequented the summer before I met Eddie. I hadn't gone into a pub on my own since that summer, but in I went. A guy behind the bar with a long ponytail served me a pint, which I took to a table in the corner. There weren't many people there, it was mid-week, and after eyeing me with mild curiosity the few who were there went back to their conversations. A copy of the previous day's *Irish Times* was lying on the table next to mine and I picked it up. Over the next two hours I spoke to no one but the bartender, who served me two more pints and a glass, without question – a fact that sent a strange thrill through me, as though I were breaking the law.

When people started to trickle in, around five-thirty, I finished my drink and left, swaying slightly on the short walk home.

That night we had a fight. Eddie came home soon after I did. He opened a bottle of wine while I cooked dinner. Almost immediately, he realized I'd been drinking. He asked me who with and I said, 'No one.'

'Alone?' he said, and I said, 'Well, I was out.'

When I told him where I'd been, he said, 'Why on earth would you go in there?'

'Why wouldn't I?'

'Well, it's not much of a way to spend an afternoon,' he said.

'I enjoyed myself.'

He rolled his eyes.

'Oh, don't be dull,' I said, in a tone I hoped was teasing.

He looked at me, puzzled. 'Is this the first time you've done that?' he said, meaning sit in the pub all afternoon. His tone was tinged with disapproval.

It *was* the first time, and yet I felt disproportionately guilty, as though this were a habit I'd kept hidden from him. I also resented his judgement, which sounded disconcertingly parental.

'What if it wasn't?' I said. 'Would you be ashamed of me?'

'Did you do something to be ashamed of?'

'I did not,' I said.

'Then what are you talking about?'

What *was* I talking about? It was my first, flailing attempt to push him away. Even in the dimness of my self-knowledge some part of me could see that. 'I don't know,' I said.

'Well, maybe you should think about it.'

'I know,' I said flatly.

'You know, you *don't* know.' He threw me a look, condescending and gently dismissive, that seemed to say he'd been put on earth to indulge me. 'Maybe you should've married one of your pals from the band.'

I looked at him. He got up from the table. I hadn't told him about that night. I could've, I hadn't done anything wrong. But maybe I wanted to see if he'd hear about it, and he had.

\*

Eddie kept me closer to him after that, at least for a while, and I didn't know whether it was out of contrition – perhaps he regretted having scolded me – or whether he was afraid I might be drifting from his orbit. It was around this time, during the third year of our marriage, the year before we moved to the house under the mountain, that we began to drink more, and there were many mornings I awoke with a sharp, thrumming pain behind my eyes and a quiver in my hands, and a feeling that we were avoiding each other's eyes.

The nights would begin pleasantly enough: we'd meet in town or drive out to the Point for an after-work pint, with a plan to come home and cook. But then we would decide to have our dinner out, and there would be wine, too much of it, and instead of going home after the meal we would go on for a late drink somewhere because – *why not?* Every now and then the night felt like a wave we could catch, reminiscent of our beginnings. But more often an edginess or a melancholy seemed to make its way into our drinking. There were times I felt I knew Eddie less well than ever, and I was shocked by whatever chutzpah, or hubris, had allowed us to undertake such an enormous thing as marriage.

There were also days that reminded me why I'd married him, days that seemed to relegate any unpleasantness or regret to the realm of temporary blindness or simple misconception. One afternoon Eddie phoned me from work and said he was coming home early and asked if I'd like to go mussel-picking at Culleenamore in Strandhill. He said we hadn't done that since our first summer, and did I remember how much I'd enjoyed it?

When we got to the beach, he reminded me how to go for the mussels lowest down on the rocks because they'd got less sun, and to choose those with the sharpest edges, as that meant they were younger. The tide was out, so that the sand banks a few hundred metres from where we picked were exposed, and in the distance we could see seals. Eddie knelt on the rocks, his trousers tucked into his rubber boots, the sleeves of an old jumper pushed up to his elbows. He was filling a bucket and I was on an adjacent rock, filling mine. When he straightened, he waved to me and smiled.

A few minutes later I heard him behind me.

'Got enough?' he said, and held out his hand for my bucket.

We climbed down on to the sand and, for whatever reason, he set both the buckets down and put his arms around me and pressed me to him. I could see over his shoulder a honey-coloured sky, the dune grass bending on the slopes. He gave my hair a tug so that my face was lifted to his and he kissed me, then he walked up the beach to where the rest of our things were while I waited with the buckets. When he came back towards me, he was looking first out to sea and then down at the sand, like a sad little boy, and I felt a wave of pity for him. It wasn't the first time, and I didn't know whether to feel alarmed or reassured, whether pity and love were mutually exclusive or whether, on the contrary, they couldn't exist without each other. As we left the beach, black clouds pushed in out of nowhere, and by the time we were on the road fat drops of rain had begun to fall and the houses either side of us were smudges in the downpour.

At home, Eddie steamed the mussels in white wine and we ate enormous bowls of them with crusty bread while the rain fell thickly beyond the sash window. Then we sprawled on the sofa, refreshed and tired from the sea air. I hadn't stopped watching him since the beach – as he was driving, as he cooked, as he uncorked the wine – and I felt as though I were witnessing something quietly spectacular. I felt in love again. I had the thought that all that was needed for us to thrive was for me to allow him to appear, even occasionally, in this light. I imagined him, not for the first time, in the distant future, and I was sure he would age into the sort of older man I had always liked the look of, weathered and sturdy and thick-set. I knew, too, that he would stick by me, and that that was not something one found easily, or cast too easily aside.

I sat up on the sofa and straddled him, and we made love like that, hardly undressing at all, hardly speaking, the taste of the sea still on us. It felt creaturely and instinctive and surprisingly gentle. Afterwards, as always, he seemed shy, so that I was left with a slightly uneasy conscience and an odd desire to protect him.

Later, in bed, I lay there in the dark, thinking that if I could only give myself to this, to Eddie, without hesitation or doubt, I could stop this struggle and begin my life in earnest. We had talked about having a child, if in a rather glancing manner – *someday*, accompanied by nervous laughter; we seemed to agree that it was the next right thing, the natural thing. We had gotten a kitten, a black-and-white female we named Olivia, and we made a disproportionate fuss over her, reporting to each other on her latest adorable antics, conversations always laced with a certain self-consciousness, as though we suspected ourselves of displaced affection, aware of what we weren't yet brave enough to do.

I turned on my side and touched my head to his shoulder. He was asleep. I imagined being pregnant with Eddie's child and felt a rush of desire that was overlaid with something unfamiliar. For an instant, I could feel myself falling under Eddie's spell again, as I had that first summer when everything was strange to me and I relied on him to interpret the world. I was sure that was what pregnancy and the early years of motherhood would mean, a deepening of my dependence on him. A wave of aversion passed through me, but so did a feeling of smugness, something I was sure I had detected time and time again in families, those sealed-off, self-regarding little units. On the one hand, they repelled me; on the other, I envied them and wanted what they had. A family, I thought. *Our* family.

In the days that followed I regarded my husband with something like submissiveness or reverence, as though I were already carrying his child and the fact had rendered me awestruck. One night in the sitting room he turned to me and said, 'We should think about buying a house,' and I clapped my hands – actually clapped them like a schoolgirl – and leapt off of my chair to join him on the sofa.

It took us six months, but one morning we found ourselves driving up the mountain road to view the house that would soon be ours. It had rained earlier, quite heavily, and now the sun was out. The mountain was a steel blue and the wet grass glinted in the light, the land so lushly green it looked irradiated. We took possession in October, and it was truer than I could have dreamed that our move to the countryside felt, if only for a while, like a return to our better selves, to that blissful first summer of our beginnings.

The day is dissolving into twilight by the time I get back to Monkstown. I've been in the house only three weeks, and already it feels like home, some part of me believing that everything I see here is the accrual of my own life, rather than the belongings of strangers.

My friend's friends bought the place in the seventies, when a lot of these seafront houses had fallen into disrepair or been divided into flats. There was no electricity in the house, and the light fittings and chandeliers had been removed, so that cables hung frayed from the ceilings. Now, the walls are lined with books; there is a closet full of china, a walled garden, kitchen drawers as big as suitcases; there are dainty, three-legged mahogany side tables, silk-covered cushions on the sofas that face the open fire. The carpets are plush and spotless. Every house on this stretch of road has undergone a similar transformation. On the next street over, a terrace of about a dozen houses, there are some days as many as six Jaguars parked. Six seems to be the full complement. I count them on my way to Tesco.

Every Thursday, a Hungarian handyman comes and, on Mondays, a Romanian woman cleans the house. Otherwise, it is just me, ascending and descending the stairs, like some historic-homes tour guide without an audience. I have never lived in a house so big, and during my first week here I aimed to spread myself among as many rooms as possible. I prowled the garden's depths, even at night. I wanted to know every corner of the place, every tree and dormant flower, each painting and book. I wanted to plunge into this accretion of family and history and nation. I imagined the precise way I would occupy each of these rooms, and the sort of person I would become as I did. In the library, I saw myself sitting by the large window in the straight-backed chair like some fusty old scholar, reading *Clarissa* and *Tristram Shandy* and all the other great works that have hovered, unread, over my life; in the enormous first-floor front room, with its broad white chaise longue, I would gaze at the sea from my reclining position, sipping tea from a china cup, as though in a period drama; in the kitchen, with its gigantic drawers of spices and pulses and exotic vinegars, I would concoct dishes I'd long meant to try but for which I'd never got round to assembling the ingredients.

Quickly, though, I found my presence contracting. I retreated from all those rooms, which is to say that I stopped imagining the lives I might live in them. Now, I occupy less and less space, though whatever space I do occupy, I occupy intensely. The house is as cold as it is beautiful, but it is more than the desire to stay warm that is behind this gathering in of self. It feels like a rather obvious metaphor – for the swift descent from the illusion of plenitude to the actuality of limits, for the way life is so effective at narrowing our horizons. A child's world is infinite not because the child is capable of realizing any dream but because the child does not yet know just how many dreams she will need to forsake, how little time and energy and fortitude will actually be available to her in this lifetime.

Now I take my air at night, my quota of two cigarettes, on

the little covered patio outside the kitchen's sliding doors, and with feet firmly planted I peer into the garden's far reaches. Beyond the end of the lawn the upper half of the Protestant church, which dominates the Crescent, looms like a giant risen from slumber, and when the night is cold and wet and the moonlight falls on the yew tree and its needles glint like tinsel, the spectacle of it all is more than satisfying – for though I lament that narrowing of world that comes with age, I know that, like all children, I overlooked much and took everything for granted, and that even into the early years of adulthood, when I thought about the world at all, in *that* way, I mistakenly assumed that all of its good, beautiful things would come around again, and then again, and again, until the time was right for me to pluck them. Now, I am old enough to know that there are people I would like to see again whom I have already seen for the last time, there are places I dream of returning to that I will never revisit, and that though a few things do come around again and offer themselves, many more do not.

When I used to visit my mother in Florida, in the time before Stan's death, before the sadness settled on her, I felt stirrings of that old sense of possibility, of the largeness of life. I would arrive at their retirement condo and lie down in the spare room, on the too-soft single mattress, between sheets I was sure I remembered from childhood, and I would feel each time the strange and sudden onset of hopefulness. It was, I thought, trace memories of youth, awakened by being back in my mother's care, of a time when I believed that the world awaited me and that its intentions were good.

Whenever I left her at the end of those visits, there lingered between and within us a longing for each other that was tender and oddly intimate, like the longing of lovers. It unnerved me slightly, this feeling, but it didn't surprise me.

She met Stan the year I went off to college. She had taken a cruise of the Pacific coast with her bridge pals. Stan was a widower and was the fifth wheel accompanying two couples, one of whom was casually acquainted with a friend of my mother's. Before they disembarked a week later back in Portland, my mother and Stan swapped numbers. One year later to the day, they married.

As they neared retirement age, a lot of their friends were relocating to Arizona, but they both loved the sea, and eventually they moved to Florida. On one of my visits to their condo, in the last months of Stan's life – I was living in Nairobi then – we were all sitting in the living room in front of our three folding tray tables, eating dinner that had been delivered from the dining room. The food was rather good, but the dinners came in individual styrofoam boxes, each food group nestled in its own compartment; even when we transferred the dinners to our plates, their components retained that air of separateness, as though wanting nothing to do with each other. Every night my mother decried the use of styrofoam. Every night we watched *Jeopardy*. It was my mother's favourite show. I used to think that if I could do one thing for her it would be to send her on a honeymoon with Alex Trebek. A cruise through the Bahamas, with lots of bridge and sunbathing and jumbo-shrimp cocktail. Alex would dote on her, wooing her with his knowledge of absolutely everything. He would draw her out, like he does with his contestants, their banal idiosyncrasies elevated, briefly, to something interesting, and my mother would feel clever and beautiful and young again.

We were just finishing our ice-cream, eating it straight from the styrofoam cups, producing together an almighty squeaking, when an ambulance and a fire engine pulled into the parking lot beneath their window. There was an astonishing amount of whirring and whooping and flashing red lights. Everything in America seemed like this to me – larger, louder, unignorable. Everything, even the Reaper's arrival, felt just a little like half-time of a football game.

I had been there a week and this was the third time this had happened.

My mother said, 'We've got a front-row seat here.' And then, sounding intrigued: 'See if you can see who it is.'

Stan heaved himself with effort from the La-Z-Boy and took the three steps towards the window. I didn't know whether to get up and join him and risk seeming prurient, or to stay where I was and risk appearing insufficiently interested in what was, after all, the central drama of their lives.

'We've got two or three people here close to a hundred years old,' Stan said to me. He said a hundred like *ahunnerd*. 'You don't get much beyond that.'

Stan had, as of that night, less than three months to live.

We rinsed our styrofoam cups and stacked them in the recycling bag. We never did see who it was being taken away. My mother went into the bedroom and lay down on her bed to read. Stan had recently bought her a Kindle. She would take it into the bedroom every night, place it beside her on the bed, then pick up her library book. She loved the public library, with its air of thrift, civic-mindedness and good intentions. But she pretended, for Stan's sake, to love her Kindle, too. She had learned how to recharge it, and this she referred to as 'using' her Kindle.

Stan's kidneys were failing. His doctor tracked their diminishing function in percentage points, as though ticking off his days to live: it amounted to the same thing. Stan had opted not to undergo dialysis, which was, I suppose, when he officially began his dying. It also marked a change in my mother. Her voice grew thinner and sometimes contained a trace of fear. Her default mood had always been one of cheerful enthusiasm. Now, on the phone, she often sounded distracted, as though she had caught sight of something approaching in the distance, something she couldn't quite make out but which she was almost certain would bring trouble.

In the days before he died, it all got much worse, dramatically so. They filled him with painkillers that made him hallucinate. He screamed at my mother and banished her from the room, as though casting out the devil.

I flew from Nairobi to be with her. Stan was still alive when I booked my ticket, he had not yet begun to writhe and shout, and there was no hint of how swiftly it would all unspool. It was Monday morning and I was due to fly on Wednesday. On Tuesday she called to tell me that he had died that morning.

I asked the questions one asks at such moments, and my mother said to me, 'You sound upset. Are you okay?'

She is in denial, I thought. She's in shock.

'Well,' I said, shaking, and a bit exasperated, 'I *am* upset. Aren't you?'

'I've done my crying,' she said calmly, as though it were an errand she had run, a very private errand, about which I should not enquire. I never understood her, but I know that she was a merciful person, and the best that I've surmised is that steeliness and a kind of keeping-at-bay steadied her through life and its vicissitudes. This was a woman who took the plots of movies seriously, and personally. She talked about the characters as though they were people she knew going morally astray. How could he *do* that? she would cry. On the other hand, she disengaged from the news. 'I try not to listen,' she told me once. 'I can't do anything about it, and it makes me sad, it makes me think civilization has gone crazy.'

With regard to my work, a *don't ask, don't tell* policy had evolved. In the beginning I had tried to share things with her, everyday things unrelated to violence or poverty. I wanted to counter the stereotypes I imagined she was burdened by. I sent her upbeat stories I had written for donors – about a disabled woman who had created her own small leather-goods business out of a shack in Trincomalee and a few hundred dollars of micro-finance, or a young Tamil who'd left Jaffna to train as a doctor in London, then given up his life of relative luxury to return to his war-torn homeland and his suffering people. But I soon realized that any picture I painted served as a foundation for envisioning more, and this she did not want to do. And so I stopped.

It shouldn't have surprised me, her refusal to imagine deeply for fear of imagining the worst – it's hardly an uncommon strategy – but it was only when Stan died that the implications of this approach revealed themselves, for better and for worse. When my mother said to me, three months after her husband's death, 'I'm surprised how much I miss him,' I got the impression her surprise was adding to the pain. I was astonished. How could she not have known? I had known. I'd been dreading, on her behalf, her aloneness. Unlike my mother, I dwell anxiously on the future, convinced that expecting the worst will render the worst less destabilizing. But the future, when it arrives, is never quite as I pictured it, and even if there is suffering, it is somehow not what I'd prepared for. I find myself as though in a dream, one of those dreams in which I realize I have studied for the wrong exam. All I have done, with my fretting and my vivid imagination about the future, is render myself miserable, yet again, in the present.

After Stan's death, my mother never really shook the air of someone going through the motions. What point was there in rallying? There were no corners of the earth she hankered to see, and nothing left to strive for. There would be no more loves, no intimate companionship, no one to partner her in the quotidian. Life had thrilled her, and I could see that it no longer did.

I passed Cauley's old bedsit the other day, not by chance. It's on the Rathmines Road, on the top floor of a terraced house of grey-brown brick. I stood at the black gate and stared up at the windows – single panes that looked like they could shatter at the slightest tap – and they were blank and lifeless. The house itself looked dead, as though nothing on earth had ever happened there.

I met Cauley in the spring of 1995.

It was late afternoon, I had just dropped Eddie at the station. He was catching the afternoon train to Dublin for a trade show. I was relieved he was going away; we both were. We had argued the night before, for the first time in ages. Things had been good with us lately. We'd spent the winter working on the house. We had stripped the kitchen wallpaper, which was oily with grime, scrubbed everything and painted. We'd sanded the sitting-room floorboards till they felt like peach fuzz, then varnished them, dizzy for days with the fumes. We had even drawn up plans for the back garden.

The argument had happened after an uneventful dinner down at a pub and restaurant in Carney, a couple of miles from home. When we'd finished eating we moved to the bar area for a nightcap, and Eddie said why didn't I come with him to Dublin the next day.

'You mean tomorrow?'

'Why not? You could go round the shops, change of scene. We could go for a meal.'

I'd been looking forward to my evening alone. 'Oh,' I said, 'I don't know. Maybe next time. We can plan it.'

'What's to plan? It's an overnight in Dublin.'

'I'm in the mood for staying home,' I said.

He shrugged. 'Suit yourself.' He sounded hurt, which surprised me. The invitation had seemed offhand; now, my refusal felt mean-spirited. I sat there reconsidering. I thought: *Why not?* I was about to say to Eddie that maybe I would come, when he began, out of the blue, to tell me a story. It was a story someone had told him recently. It concerned a man who was having an affair. His wife knew. It was an agonizing time. When the man would go off to whatever city his lover was in, the wife would pack his case for him, as she always had – he was someone who travelled a lot. She said that just because he was behaving like a monster was no reason for her to change her habits. It was both a strategy for containment and a way of retaining her equilibrium in the face of uncertainty and possible disaster. Whoever had told Eddie the story thought the wife was a fool, but Eddie disagreed. He said it took a lot of spine to do that, and a lot of wisdom, and he bet anything the marriage would survive.

It was a strange story for Eddie to tell. He wasn't prone to mulling over the nature of other people's intimacies or pondering abstractions.

Naturally, I asked him if he was having an affair.

He shook his head, his eyes thrown heavenward. 'Of course not.'

'Then what are you talking about?'

'I'm just telling you a story,' he said.

'About the kind of wife you want me to be?'

He said why did everything have to be about me, and I said that it didn't but that clearly there was a moral to the story, and he crossed his arms and looked around the bar, which meant he wanted to move on.

We talked about other things – the trade show, and a piece I was researching on the seaweed industry, and what we might do over the weekend. And then, because we'd had too much to drink, I went back to that story. I wouldn't let it go. I became convinced it was apocryphal, something Eddie had made up in order to warn me or to impart a lesson. I told him I could see right through it, what he was trying to tell me.

'You're being ridiculous,' he said.

I straightened up on my stool and said self-righteously, 'Am I?'

'Let's go home.'

'*Am* I?'

He got up and nodded towards the door, then headed for it, expecting me to follow.

I sat, in a show of childish defiance, but when he opened the door without looking back, I followed.

He put the key in the ignition but didn't start the car. Instead, he heaved a huge sigh and said that sometimes he had no idea what I wanted from him.

The sudden collapse of his anger confused me. Because I didn't know what else to say, I said that I was sorry, but it came out sounding more exasperated than contrite. He stared straight ahead for a moment at the windscreen, then he turned the key and we drove home in silence.

In the morning, a drab light came through the Velux window. Eddie was asleep, his face towards the opposite wall but his body turned partly towards me, one arm bent under him. He looked like someone who had fallen from a height, whose body was twisted in ways that can mean only one thing. In the far corner of the bedroom, where the laundry always piled up, were our clothes from the previous night. There was a lamp one of us had set temporarily on a pile of hardbacks and its shade was askew. Eddie's small suitcase, which had only a can of shaving foam and a pair of boxers in it, was yawning open on the floor. Everything looked random, and careless, and I had the thought that I was doing it all wrong, that I had been from the start, as though I'd been playing a game whose rules I had entirely misunderstood.

In the afternoon I left him to the station, then went to town for groceries. It was one of those lifeless, grey days when all you see are plastic shopfronts and skids of dog shit. Where the footpath met the bridge, a drunk was standing. He stood there like a sentry at Buckingham Palace, like he wouldn't budge if you paid him. His few strands of silver hair had been combed neatly across his head. His face was empurpled and large-pored from drink, and his nose was swollen, its tip gnarled like a root. But he had that unlikely air of dignity that certain drunks have – purposeful and upright and very fragile. I thought if I said, *Boo!* his very heart would shatter. I nodded to him in greeting, and he smiled back, glassy-eyed, a very small and knowing smile, almost priestly but for its humility.

I was halfway up the path between the two bridges when

I spotted Kevin, a guy Eddie and I sometimes talked to at the pub, coming towards me. I stopped. We exchanged the usual cascade of banalities, and then he said that his old friend Cauley was due around six and why didn't I join them in Mulligan's for a drink?

'Eddie's away,' I said. I thought it might be awkward without him. I didn't know Kevin well.

'But *you're* not.' He was smiling, but there was something behind it, a slight smirk.

We looked down at the river. It was low tide and I could see a couple of car tyres, a single shoe lying forlornly on its side, a mangled umbrella. I had a perverse fascination for the detritus on the river bank. Today there was also a package of processed meat, unopened, and nearby a naked doll, an arm and a leg locked in goose step. Big white swans slumbered on the gravel, their bodies spreading fatly, their heads lying inert on their backs, something disconcerting and suggestive in those long, limp, supine necks of theirs. When they lifted off from the surface of the water, their wings made a great *thwock*ing sound, and on a day of low spirits, a day like today, I found them creatures of particular menace.

I looked at my watch. It was five-thirty. I felt suddenly impatient for six o'clock. 'I'll come for one,' I said.

I already knew a bit about Cauley. He and Kevin had been friends since they were boys, and Kevin had once suggested that we should meet because we were both in radio, though I was with the rinky-dink local station and Cauley was getting gigs on a national station. I knew that Cauley came from a little town in the midlands, where his father still lived, and that his mother had decamped to Dublin and was with another man. Cauley lived in Dublin now, too, but he was known down our way because an aunt of his had married a local man, and together they ran a shop and petrol station out on the Donegal road. Growing up, Cauley had spent summers with them, and that was how he and Kevin knew each other.

His first name was Darragh but everybody called him by his surname. When he turned up at Mulligan's, Kevin introduced us and he shook my hand. It wasn't the firmest of grips and his palm was a bit sweaty. I was ready to be defensive, even cutting, because I expected him to be full of himself. He was twenty-eight years old. He had just had his first play staged at the Peacock in Dublin and was working on a film script, for which he'd reportedly gotten a nice lump of development money. I had heard him on radio, reviewing films or theatre productions in London, and he was good – rapid-fire, excited, but with a hint of the sardonic. Instead of trying to hide the country accent, he sometimes thickened it, as a kind of *fuck you* to all the formal education and privilege that had not been his.

What kind of a picture can I paint of him? He was tall, by Irish standards, but thick-set, with a kind of hunkering quality that could make him look furtive and up-to-no-good, even when he was neither. He had a funny way of walking – always rushing, the very picture of someone running late, but with an odd, loping stride, as though he were walking a dog, one of those monsters that jerk their owners along, or as though he had himself on a lead, which I imagine was often how he felt. His skin was fair, it flushed a baby-pink in the heat. He was not, in other words, dashing. But he had a pent-up quality, a hunger, and an obvious intelligence. He had a habit, during lulls in the conversation, of chewing his lips with an intensity that looked capable of drawing blood, and when he smoked I sometimes saw a tremble in his hand. His response to this tangle of anxieties was to behave as though he had nothing to lose, and that recklessness seemed to me, and perhaps still does, a form of courage.

Would I call him a drunk? Not quite. That would be to suggest a certain sloppiness, a lack of focus or the living of a lie, and none of those things quite applied. To spend time with Cauley was to watch someone throw himself at life, someone who happened to drink a lot. Even when sitting still, or as still as he ever got, he churned; he had the compression of a piston, one of those guys who's always got one leg juddering under the table.

We sat three in a row on high stools, the kind with no arms and whose slippery vinyl seats puff like a risen loaf. Before I could say anything Cauley told me he'd read something I'd written in a Sunday paper. It was about a young woman from the town who had been sexually assaulted and whose attacker had gotten off on a technicality. The girl had given me an interview. Cauley knew both the families involved and said that the guy's brother had done worse two years ago and the girl had been too scared to press charges.

'The same girl?'

'A friend of hers.'

'I didn't know that.'

'Well,' he said, 'there's no reason you would.'

I felt foolish. I was the one who lived here, I'd interviewed the girl, and he knew more than I did. Not that I could've done anything with the other story, but the fact that no one had mentioned it to me made me feel I was out of my depth.

Cauley caught my discomfort. 'They're savages, that family. Nobody knows the half of what they've done.'

And then he peered, pointedly, into my almost-empty glass, and I said okay to another drink.

By the time he was making his way back from the bar, two other people had squeezed into the space beside me. Someone was talking to me but I was watching Cauley, who was holding my eye as he wormed through the knot of people between us. He handed me the pint and I leaned forward to say something, and the heel of my boot caught on the rung of the stool and I started to slip off the vinyl seat.

He steadied me, his hand just above my hip, and said, 'Whoa!'

I was gripping his shoulder.

'Shall we move to a table?' he said.

More people had arrived – there were now eight or ten in our group – and we crowded into one of the U-shaped booths with the hard, mud-brown benches. Cauley scooted in beside me, and soon another round appeared. The night was reaching the stage where there was much pointless clamour and the half-serious slapping of palms on tables for emphasis. In the hubbub, Cauley and I pressed closer. We talked about Dublin, and where he'd grown up, about childhood summers in Sligo and about his parents, who were still technically married but had nothing to do with one another.

'My parents were never married,' I said, by way of solidarity. And then added, as though the second fact somehow followed from the first: 'I'm married.'

Cauley nodded and lifted his brows slightly, as if what I'd said was too obvious or uninteresting to warrant a response. It was the first time I'd referred to Eddie, but it was clear that Cauley knew about him. It was always like that there – you'd meet someone for the first time and get the sense that they'd been briefed on you. We sat in silence for a moment, childishly glum, until at last he leaned away from me and cocked his head to one side and said in his camped-up country accent, 'And, how *is* it, being married?'

We were drunk by then, and I stared at the table for a dramatically long time and murmured, in a tone so woebegone it shames me still, 'I wouldn't know any more.'

'Ho!' he said, then gave his head a quick shake as though to clear it.

Cauley was always saying things like 'Ho!' and 'Mighty!', always exclaiming, always ironic. He looked me briefly in the eye, just a glance. Then he put his arm over the back of the bench behind me, pressed his thigh to mine and leaned across me to say something to Kevin, who was sitting the other side of me. I felt the heat of him, a sudden strong pull. I picked up the merest scent of sweat. I leaned my head back against his arm and let them talk.

At some point, I saw that Cauley had fished a pen from the

inside pocket of his suit jacket and was scribbling an address on a scrap of paper. Underneath the address he wrote a telephone number. Then he clicked the pen and tucked it smartly back into his pocket. It was only then I noticed how out of place his big-city after-work outfit was. It was April, but down the country we were all still in our winter woollies and jeans, and in that jacket Cauley looked like a boy playing dress-up. Poor Cauley. He was only just becoming himself at the time, or trying to, and it was a hit-and-miss process. But he was out there in the world and you could tell that he was proud, and it touched me. He handed me the bit of paper and said, 'Here's how to get hold of me.'

At closing time, we stumbled out on to O'Connell Street. The crowd from inside was milling about on the footpath. There was a spring frost, and after the smoke and stink of indoors the sharp night air felt as clean and other-worldly as if we'd stepped out on to a mountaintop.

Cauley rested his head for a moment on the shelf of my shoulder, puppyish and awkward. 'Ring me,' he said, in a voice so hushed and intimate I half thought I'd imagined it.

Then he lifted his head, squeezed my hand and called out his goodbyes, and off he went, in a terribly self-conscious saunter, one hand in his trouser pocket, the other swinging slightly at his side. He knew I was watching and he was striving for just the right effect but, poor Cauley, he had no idea what the right effect was, let alone how to achieve it.

I met a Somali on the Liffey boardwalk today. It was one of those fine, blue winter afternoons you so rarely get here, cool but hardly a breeze. There was something so still and perfect about it that it felt sorrowful, the sort of day you'd call to mind if you were leaving this world behind. I was dressed warmly enough that I decided to sit outside along the river, at one of the high tables beside the coffee kiosk on Ormond Quay. A few gaunt junkies sat on the benches, and I eyed them furtively and with some amazement. On a wet, dreary day they look not so very different from a lot of Dublin's pallid and bedraggled foot traffic. But on a clean, clear day they can seem another form of life entirely, slithered up from the deep and unaccustomed to the light.

A briny smell was coming off the river, which was a milky green in the sun, and on the railing seagulls squalled and the pigeons gulped like turkeys. Two suitcases being wheeled along the footpath sounded like a squad of jack-booted soldiers approaching. When the din faded, I heard his voice. He and his companion spoke first in Somali – a rapid-fire paddle of words, as though they were barking urgent orders at each other – and then in English, ordering coffee. A dart of nostalgia passed through me, as though it were my own native tongue I was hearing, and when he turned around, I said, 'Are you Somali?'

He was from Baidoa, in the south of the country. I told him that I had been to Baidoa, and he was surprised, but not shocked. Everywhere thinks that it's the centre of the universe. I invited him and his friend to join me. His friend knocked back his espresso and said that he was going, but Ahmed stayed behind. He asked me who I'd worked for and what I was doing now, and I told him that I had spent the better part of the last four years reading field reports from Gedo and Mogadishu and Kismayo, and that I was now writing a report on Dadaab. I took pleasure in pronouncing the place names, because I knew that it gave him pleasure to hear them, but also because it connected me to a part of my life I'd left behind.

Ahmed was tall, with fine features and long arms and fingers, and the beginnings of a pot belly. He left Somalia nine years ago, going first to Dadaab, then to London, then coming here. He told me he has a wife and three children. The family lives in an apartment up the far end of the quays, near the National Museum.

I asked the obvious. 'Do you miss it?'

'Never,' he said, matter-of-factly. 'We are better off here.'

'You could still miss it,' I said, 'even if you're better off.'

Ahmed smiled. 'Yes, but then you wouldn't be very smart.'

I laughed. I have met many refugees and immigrants, and in my experience they tend to fall into one of two categories: those who never get over the severing, the expulsion, who carry with them the air of rupture, as though it is a limb they've lost; and those, like Ahmed, who walk straight into the future and don't look back, something in them cauterized.

We sipped our coffee and talked about Dublin and Ahmed's job as a taxi driver. I've heard reports of white drivers on the ranks refusing to move their cars up to let African drivers in. But Ahmed said the work was fine.

'I mind my own business. I take my fares.' He shrugged. 'Irish people, they're like people anywhere.'

'Is that a good thing?'

He looked at me. 'What do you think?'

I told him how I used to love the taxi rides to and from the airport in Nairobi, and he squinted – perplexed, I thought, by what my sentimentality alighted on. It was true, though. When I thought of the things I missed about there, I thought of being in the back of a taxi at dawn, heading out the Mombasa road for a flight to Somalia, when the city was only beginning to stir. On the verges along the highway there'd be people walking, probably miles, to work, and over the time it took the taxi to reach the airport the numbers moving towards the city would have swelled to the point where it looked as though a great migration was under way.

At the airport, boarding the Beechcraft, I always felt I was leaving the world behind. I felt like an astronaut. Once in-country, we flew on even smaller planes, with bench seats. From the windows we could see the desiccated earth, distressingly near, goats scattering under the roar and shadow of our gleaming machine. On one of my last trips, I'd been to Wajid, in south-central Somalia, not far from Ahmed's home place. I was reporting on two programmes my office had recently begun supporting. I'd had one of those days, by which I don't mean the best sort of day or the worst but rather the kind that would once have been inconceivable to me, the kind that make me imagine a little game. In the game I am shown an image, from the distant future, of just such an unprecedented day, and I have to guess how I got there and what's going on. I like this game, even if I can play it only retroactively, already knowing the answers, because it reminds me that there is a future full of people I've yet to encounter and moments worth waiting for. It reminds me that I know very little, in fact, about my life, and even less about the world itself.

It was my third day in Wajid, and I was sitting in a class-room with about twenty adolescent girls wearing brightly coloured headscarves. At the front of the class were two teachers, a woman named Amino and a man named Abdi. On a flip chart Amino had sketched an erect penis, with testicles in the inadvertent shape of a heart. The penis dripped ejaculate in the direction of a chute, which blossomed, flute-shaped, into the roomier chamber of a uterus.

Amino was explaining, in Somali, how pregnancy occurred. Pregnancy wasn't the half of it, though. We had just watched a video made by members of the Somali dias-pora in Denmark campaigning against female genital mutilation, which was the real focus of the day. If statistics were accurate, about 95 per cent of the girls in the class-room could expect to suffer it. Some might simply have the tip of the clitoris snipped off, but most would have the full treatment: total removal of the clitoris and labia minora and the sewing together of the labia majora, just a small opening left for urine and menstrual flow. Nearly all of them would be operated on with unsterilized instruments and without anaesthesia. When the girls married, they would have to be recut, through thickened scar tissue, to enable intercourse.

I had met both Abdi and Amino before class. We'd sat outside on the concrete step and Abdi had told me about his wife. He held out his hand and ran an index finger over the smooth skin of his palm and said, 'This is what it was like.' He was referring to her vagina, sewn nearly shut. He had travelled with her to Baidoa before their wedding to find a doctor who could open her up again without mutilating her further. He described her first pregnancy, three days of labour that ended in a stillbirth. Unlike a lot of men I met in Somalia, Abdi didn't view the situation as part of the natural order of things. He found it barbaric and wanted to change it. Abdi was an instinctive feminist, meaning he had come by his ideas not because of some NGO training course but because he had an inborn conviction that people, men and women, had a right to life, to security, to bodily integrity.

As for Amino, she was running a safe house for women who suffered from fistula – a condition that can result from prolonged obstructed labour caused by genital mutilation, in which a hole opens between a woman's vagina and her bladder or rectum, and which results in incontinence and infertility. A lot of women with fistula were abandoned by their husbands and shunned by their communities. Just then, Amino had four women living with her, wearing diapers and awaiting transport to Addis for reconstructive surgery. Before class, we had visited the house. A satellite dish was beaming a tennis match, on mute, into the large living area, which contained three sofas covered by floral throws. It was mid-morning, and the room was shadowy and cool. Now and then, one or another of the women would drift through the room. Every time they passed the sofa where we were sitting, we exchanged wan smiles. Only Amino spoke to me, and as she did, and as I looked around, I was filled with both utter despair and a feeling of being in the presence of absolute goodness: the ideal of compassion and rationality embodied.

After class, Amino and Abdi walked me to the courtyard, where the driver, Hassan, was waiting. A child – the driver's daughter, who looked to be seven or eight and was in another class in the school – was standing beside him. She buried her face in his trouser leg as we approached, then slowly, flirtatiously, peek by peek, emerged.

She told me her name was Waris. Her hair was cropped short and her features were delicate but strong, and perfectly symmetrical. She had large, almond-shaped eyes and a playful, teasing manner. I imagined her a bit older, visiting an uncle or aunt in New York, spotted by a modelling agency's scout while queuing at a Burger King. I thought of my guess-the-future game – Waris ten years from now, gazing out a window over Central Park West, wondering what had hit her.

The next afternoon I caught the return flight to Nairobi. The city looked, as all cities do from the air, exposed and easily destructible, and I felt a surge of tenderness for the whole teeming, illogical, fucked-up world. In the taxi, the driver asked where I'd come from, and I said Somalia. The reaction was always the same. The driver gave a little cluck and raised his eyebrows, and remarked on whatever the latest scrap of news or rumour was – that day it was the question of whether Ethiopian forces were going to pull out of Somalia – and I felt as though I had returned from a place of quarantine, where everything has gone awry and all the talk is of containment. In Nairobi, the guns were mostly hidden, and the landscape was so lush compared to the cracked earth of Somalia, and driving away from the low-slung airport, I could nearly feel the trees inhaling and exhaling, the warm breath of them. I was back on terra firma, and there seemed nowhere on earth as beautiful, as civilized, as reliable, as Jomo Kenyatta airport and the city that lay beyond.

I asked Ahmed about Dadaab, and he said that he and his wife had been there for seven months, and that a relative in London had sponsored them for resettlement. Seven months was good. A lot depended on timing, which countries had agreed to take how many people at a given time, and where you happened to be, geographically and in the asylum process, when things started to flow.

'You're lucky,' I said, and immediately felt foolish for saying it. But I was thinking of the country he'd escaped, with its pointless, repetitive cycles of violence, which resemble nothing so much as active addictions. I was thinking of Hamdi, too, who had set herself on fire in the camp. I thought of the men who had paid her for sex and how some of those same men would've called for her execution had she been caught prostituting. I wondered what kind of a man Ahmed was. I wished I could think of a single question to ask him that would tell me whether he was like Abdi in Wajid or whether, instead, he would've joined the men in condemning Hamdi.

'Do you ever go home for a visit?' I asked.

He was gazing across the river to the far side, at the maw of Temple Bar and the traffic, which was at a standstill. He shook his head.

'You don't want to?'

'I'm not homesick,' he said. 'All my family are here, or dead.'

Maybe that was it, I thought, maybe place meant nothing to him, only people. I wanted him to talk some more, I wanted just to hear him. Why? I have no love for where he came from, certainly no claim on it; it was only my own life it reminded me of, and hardly its most cheerful period. But he didn't say anything more. He got up, stretched his long arms up over his head, and said goodbye.

I sat for a while longer, just watching, everything made rich with sunlight, and the city gone a little hushed, as it does on such days. I thought about Harry, of something he said to me the last time I saw him. We've been meeting up every couple of weeks, for coffee or lunch. It's a friendship based, ostensibly, on work, but I know that it's also about Harry knowing I'm on my own and a bit adrift, and maybe liking the idea that he's keeping an eye on me. Last week, for the first time, we went for dinner, and maybe it was that – the fact that it was evening, and everything felt that much less like it had anything to do with work – that made him open up about his life. He started talking about the many moves he'd made over the years and all the travelling, which his marriage had not survived. He said the irony was that, as his work had become focused on trying to settle people, migrants and refugees and the displaced, his own life had become more peripatetic, so that by the time he finally came back to Dublin nowhere felt like home, or maybe everywhere did, just a little. He wanted to believe that he'd gained more than he'd lost in that transaction, that in becoming less exclusive in his attachments he'd come to feel a deeper kind of affection for the world. He said there was always a rupture when you left a place, until you realized it had to do with the person you had somehow decided to be. Until you saw that you carried all these rifts and partings with you, like you carried scars, and that instead of feeling like things torn from you, they were part of you.

I like this idea. I like Harry. He calms me. He has a way of expanding the view. Panning out, and out, into a panorama. It's not that the view is all good – Harry is essentially a pessimist. It's just that there's a sense of perspective. I think he has lost a lot and survived, though I don't know what exactly I'm referring to. Apart from the limitations on his mobility, Harry's losses seem not greater than most. He has, in many ways, a rather nice life. But I get the sense he's made peace with himself, and that it took some doing, and that he's emerged from that battle wistful, bemused, a little elsewhere. He watches the world as though it were a far-away thing and he a minor god made melancholy by us humans, by the fact that we never, ever, seem to learn.

Over dinner, he said that if we don't know where we belong, we can feel homesick for almost anywhere we've been.

I thought then of the place I'd lived in Nairobi, a cottage on the grounds of a larger house. The cottage was lovely — parquet floors and hardwood furnishings and breezes drifting through the ornate iron grilles set across the windows. But in the evenings, or the middle of the night, I could sometimes hear gunshots in the distance, and the week after my mother died my next-door neighbour was badly beaten during a burglary. The neighbour wasn't a friend, I had never met her or even seen her — the walls between properties were high and when you entered your own drive it was through solid metal gates that a guard pulled closed behind you. The guards patrolled the grounds throughout the night, their boots swishing through the grass, and even if they were trustworthy, which I believed ours to be, I was made uneasy by the fact of men circling in the darkness and I rarely slept well in that house.

By day, I felt only marginally freer. The gardens on the property were lush and varied, and outside the cottage I had my own small patch of lawn and herbs and flowers, bordered by a low brick wall and furnished with a stone-topped table and two rattan chairs. But I could never quite bring myself to sit out there, not without a cringing self-consciousness, and I never touched the garden. It was clear that everything that grew on the property belonged, in its way, to Dixon. Dixon was the gardener, and he despised me. He had from the day I moved in. I didn't take it personally. I knew it wasn't *me* he disliked. And he knew that I knew. We understood each other. We understood that I could never sufficiently atone for acts that I myself had not committed but of which I had been, in whatever vague or concrete way, the beneficiary. So while Dixon ambled loosely about the grounds, a pair of long shears or a clump of just-cut stalks hanging from his hand, his stare cold and dead, I sat at my kitchen table and gazed dolefully out the window at the trumpet flowers and the birds of paradise, like a sickly child who couldn't risk the out-of-doors.

I told Harry about a certain strange day in Nairobi. I was walking down the street towards that cottage with the parquet floors and the garden I couldn't touch and the gardener who loathed me – a place where I had not known peace and that I thought often of leaving – and as I looked towards the solid grey gate that would open to admit me, I felt a wave of nostalgia break in me. I had projected myself spontaneously into the future, a future in which I looked back on this house, on this unhappy time, and saw it all through the soft focus of recollection, and – lo! – it grew lovely.

I said to Harry that my immediate impulse had been to figure out how to repeat the trick, so as more often to enjoy this terrible, crushing tenderness for the present.

Harry laughed. 'Mind that,' he said. 'Beware of attachment.' Harry is a bit of a Buddhist.

I said, 'Come on, try it, close your eyes. Say it's six months in the future, and you are remembering right now.'

'Okay,' he said gamely, and we closed our eyes.

I don't know how long I kept mine closed – a minute,

maybe two; it was hard to judge the time. Sounds differentiated themselves amidst the clatter and din of the restaurant — a door opening and closing, the rise and fall of voices, the thump of a cork pulled from a wine bottle. I heard Harry shift in his seat. I heard my own breathing. I became aware of what felt like a very faint, very subtle electric current in my body and a twitchiness around my eyes. I tried not to feel self-conscious, but at a certain point I had the sudden funny fear that Harry wasn't at the table any more, and I opened my eyes again. He was there, sitting very still in his chair, his eyes open, watching me. I stared at him, surprised. He blinked a couple of times and hesitated, before looking away. Neither of us said another word about it.

It was mid-May the first time I visited Cauley. The day was eerily still, with a flat, unvarying heat. We were in his bedsit, with the sash window raised. The lace curtains hung greyish and unmoving. We had just made love, and Cauley was sleeping, fitfully. Every so often his mouth would twitch, or he would jut his chin out quickly and part his dry lips and wet them with the tip of his tongue, before turning his head to the side and nestling it into the pillow, as though consoling himself.

It had been three weeks since the night we were introduced in Sligo. I had written him a circumspect note saying that I would likely be in Dublin on such and such a date and perhaps we might meet for a drink, upon which he had sent a note to the house. I'd been in town that day and come home with Eddie, and when we walked through the door it was Eddie who picked the post up off the floor of the entryway. He sifted through it and handed two letters to me, one a bank statement and the other a hand-addressed envelope, which I opened with idle curiosity rather than excitement. At that moment, I wasn't thinking of Cauley. Had I been, I might've been better prepared when Eddie said to me, 'What's that?'

There was no accusation in his tone, no reason for there to be, and he was still perusing some letter of his own, but he must've sensed my absorption, because he looked up at me then, with concern, wondering if I'd received bad news.

'Oh,' I said, shaking my head, as though puzzled to be receiving the letter. 'It's from Kevin's friend. The journalist who lives in Dublin.' I had mentioned Cauley to Eddie after meeting him, I had told him that Cauley said he could introduce me to someone at the *Irish Times*. I was calculating, in case Cauley's name came up later, that it wouldn't seem strange. But I hadn't said I'd written to him.

'The one who works for the *Irish Times*?' Eddie said.

'He doesn't work for them, but he knows people who do. He writes plays,' I said, then added, 'I think.' I hadn't even told my first lie and I could feel my throat constricting.

'What's his name?' Eddie said, but he'd already gone back to reading his own letter.

'His name is Darragh Cauley.'

The note read simply, *Yes, it would be good to meet up, I have a few ideas of people I can introduce you to. Let's arrange a time. Mornings best to ring me.* D

Underneath, he'd written the phone number again, the same one he'd given me the first night.

I put the letter in my bag and went into the living room. For something to do, I picked up Olivia and lifted her so that her legs swung free, and I pressed my head to hers until she squirmed.

From the kitchen, Eddie called, 'The *Irish Times* would be good.'

The next morning, I phoned Cauley. One week later, we met. I was in Dublin to interview a man who was the head psychologist of an Alzheimer's unit at a hospital in Stillorgan. I sat there listening to that man, who was dignified and a little wearied, knowing that, behind him, in rooms padded for safety, people were growing ever more frail and demented, and I'd felt a terrible thrill about the likelihood that I would soon be making love. When the interview ended and we'd toured what we could of the unit, and the man was bidding me goodbye, I had the urge to go tearing from the hospital lobby out into the car park, to toss my folder in the air and, as the papers scattered to the wind, flee towards the land of the living.

Cauley and I had agreed to meet at a pub on the Rathmines Road. I'm sure we both knew we'd go to his place, but Cauley was afraid to sound presumptuous by suggesting I meet him there. I was about twenty yards from the pub when I spotted him sauntering up the footpath from the opposite direction, affecting what was meant to look like nonchalance.

When he saw me coming, he smiled and waved, a simple, undisguised happiness in his expression. He walked towards me, parodying the very air of cool he'd been trying just a moment ago to project. I laughed.

'Hiya!' he said, and kissed me on the cheek.

'Hiya.'

'Hi,' he said, softer now.

He'd got his hair cut since I'd seen him last. It made him look boyish, and though I was only a few years older than he, I had a moment of misgiving, as though I were defiling him. When I remarked on the haircut he said goofily, 'Gerry's finest, three quid.'

We looked at the door of the pub, but neither of us moved to go in. He asked if I was hungry.

'I ate at the hospital,' I said.

He made a face. 'That must've been tasty.'

'A cheese sandwich,' I said. 'Nothing adventurous.'

'I have food at my place. It's just around the corner. Or we could go out somewhere. Or do you want a drink?'

'Show me your place,' I said.

There was none of the usual song and dance. I had no reason to be cagey, or coy. Marriage makes utilitarians of us, and adultery, which pretends to such risk and adventure, requires no courage – because whether I put it plainly to myself or not, I'd known, as I set out that day to meet Cauley, that whatever happened I need not sleep alone that night. If in the aftermath I wanted to flee him, or if he went all funny on me, I would be protected from that grim post-coital loneliness by the very institution I was betraying.

It is often difficult to remember, once a thing has happened, what you had expected of it. But I do remember being surprised. I suppose I had expected a certain awkwardness, or hesitancy, a deference, even. But when we entered Cauley's room it was as though a switch had been flipped and he was sure, suddenly, of everything. He was hungry, animalistic, shameless; he was everywhere at once. All tongue and teeth and hands, a hard thigh wedging its way between my thighs, a finger gliding in and out like a slow piston along the flat of my tongue while he looked me square in the eye, his own mouth slightly agape. I had fleeting thoughts, as we made our way, stumbling, across the room, as we shucked our clothes and shimmied free of our undergarments, that I had misread him entirely. But they were only fleeting. There are very few people who, if we've observed them closely, will actually surprise us when the time comes. Anyway, I don't think he was sure of anything. It was only desire, with its air of the irrefutable.

The roughness of his jaw chafed my face. That surprised me, too. I had assumed he would be rather soft and hairless, what with that peach-pink skin and his hands, which still had a slight childish pudginess to them. So I didn't expect to find whorls of mannish hair, rather a lot of it. It had the look of having been flung there, something random and indiscriminate about it, and it caused in me an odd stab of pity.

Something else about Cauley: he was generous. I don't mean that he was excessively tender or solicitous, or particularly systematic in his ministrations. More that nothing human was foreign to him, which gave me permission to be myself, whoever that might be. So while a part of me revelled in it – biting his lip and shuddering at the probe and squelch of his fingers, all that arch-backed bucking and the throaty sighs, the theatrics of sex that you sometimes wonder if you learned from the movies – there was another part witnessing it with a kind of shock, as though I were seeing myself clearly for the first time.

Afterwards we lay face to face, gazing at each other, stupefied and a little frightened, as though each of us had created the other entire, out of thin air. It was early evening. From the street below came the sounds of rush hour. The traffic had picked up noticeably; you could hear the groan and hiss of buses, the squeal of brakes, an occasional shout or laugh, a car door slamming. But it all seemed very far away, like a memory of such sounds.

I began to look around the room, to take note of his life as he'd arranged it, and I saw that it, too, was not as I'd imagined. I had expected to enter the bedsit and see a mess, vehement and male – heaps of dirty clothes, empty beer bottles, unwashed dishes and tea towels stiff with mopped-up spills. I'd pictured a small television with a smudged screen, and resting atop it a half-full mug of ancient, greying tea; books and pens and spiral notebooks strewn across the floor like toys that needed picking up; a mushroomy smell rising from a laundry basket.

Instead, I saw his few dress shirts and trousers hanging from a metal frame on wheels. Lined up precisely under the bottom rod were three pairs of shoes. There was the bed, which we were lying on, and a dull brown love seat with a wood-laminate coffee table in front of it. There was a bed-side table with a well-scratched surface. The kitchen was a sink in the corner with a rusted white immersion tank sus-pended over it, a small draining board, a waist-high fridge and a portable two-hob gas cooker.

In the corner of the room that did not contain the kitchen or the love seat or the bed was a rectangular fold-up table, the same brown as the lumpy little sofa, which I imagined jiggled slightly as he worked at it. On the table was an Amstrad, a printer, a stack of clean A4 paper, three more stacks that were successive drafts of the screenplay, and a play in progress. There were two unopened bottles of red wine on a ledge behind the table, and another one, two thirds drunk, with the cork pressed neatly into its neck, beside the Amstrad. The one small note of disorder – a coffee cup listing in a cereal bowl from that morning's breakfast – had the look of something waiting to be remonstrated with and removed.

I wondered how I could've been so wrong, not only about how he lived but about the aftermath of our encounter. I had imagined that it would bring me to my senses, remind me that I was a grown-up now, with a cupboard full of wedding china and candlesticks that matched. I had thought that if we did manage to linger, half naked, over a glass of corked wine, it would be brief and awkward, and that when enough time had passed that I could leave without seeming over-hasty or putting too clear a stamp of failure on the thing, I would gather my clothes from their improbable locations around the room, and I would go downstairs and hail a taxi and make my way to the train station, feeling rueful and cinematic. On the train home, passing through the dull midlands that never failed to dispirit me, by which time the whole episode would have begun to feel unreal, I would offer myself some sad congratulations, because whether I'd honestly believed it or not in the run-up – the bit about being brought back to my senses – it had turned out to be true.

But I knew, as I lay there in Cauley's bed, looking around the room and hearing the soft stutter of his breathing beside me, that it had not turned out to be true. I knew that when he woke there would be no embarrassment between us. Already I was thinking of when I might see him again.

The first time I looked out my third-floor window here I thought of a tsunami. I thought: *If a tsunami hits, I will be safe.* I saw myself herding people up the stairs to the highest ground, where we would crowd round the windows and watch as our world was transfigured – the trains flung free of the tracks, cars smashed against the terraced houses, trees sucked from the ground – and then the sea pulling back into itself, as though innocent of the destruction. For decades I have had a recurring nightmare in which a monstrous swell rises up but is arrested in the moment before breaking. Sometimes I am on the shore, watching people float, tinily, atop this wall of water that is on the verge of collapsing catastrophically on to the beach. Other times I am in the water myself when the sea grows terrifyingly tall, and it is not the fear of drowning I become aware of but the vast abyss beneath me.

I was afraid that living in this house would prompt those nightmares, but not once since moving in have I dreamed of the sea in any state.

Instead, I dream of Eddie. The dreams seem to have come out of nowhere. Years went by when, though I might've thought of him from time to time, he never breached the barrier between my conscious and my sleeping mind. Now that he has, I find myself curious when I lie down at night, as though there is a life we might yet live out together, realizable only in dreams. The other night, we arranged to be remarried – to each other, I mean. The ceremony was due to begin, I was in the front garden of our house, the guests were already arriving, when I realized – in the way you do in dreams, when you 'discover' something you've already done – that I had called off the wedding. Eddie knew, but I hadn't told anyone else. I started to panic about the impending humiliation, the disappointment everyone would feel in me. And then Eddie arrived, looking strong and sure and handsome. He was wearing the suit and tie he'd worn at our actual wedding, and he had already taken care of things: he had told the guests that it was off. He put his arm around me and uttered one of those inane lines that seem perfectly sensible within the dream. 'It's okay,' he said, 'they want us to go on the blue bus with them.' I leaned into him and said, 'I love you, I love you so much.' And off we strolled, arm in arm, like one of those not-so-young couples you see in ads for retirement plans.

The line dividing sea from sky is blurred today, and the world looks naïve and precarious, as though painted by children. Between my window and the sea there is an expanse of about three hundred feet that is comprised of the sea road, the train-station car park, the tracks and the retaining wall beyond. As the tide moves in and the water level rises with a speed that looks unnatural, an insupportable anxiety is triggered in me. I can see the railings that stand between the tracks and the sea but I cannot see the land beneath – the dun-coloured beach, rippled and unpretty, or the desultory outcropping of rock beyond – and the station and the intermittent trains appear to be floating.

This uneasy fascination with the sea has been with me since childhood. Every summer when I was growing up we visited my grandparents at their vacation place down the Oregon coast at Agate Beach. The house was a three-bedroom clapboard with a wooden porch that they rented out when they weren't in it – humble in comparison to the fancy vacation homes that were slowly growing up around them. It sat high on a bluff, and to get to the beach we had to descend a pine-shaded, zigzagging path that opened on to a huge expanse of white sand beach which seemed, in its suddenness, like a moment out of a fairy tale, the very embodiment of possibility and wonder. Fog could roll in without warning, though, and often a bright, clear morning would turn misty and damp within minutes, so that a slight anxiety attended even the finest of days, a watchfulness that I often think persists in people who have grown up in fickle climates.

The Pacific at that latitude was cold, but my mother used to plunge in regardless, gliding like a seal, her head held stiffly above the swell, as I knelt digging in the sand beside my grandparents, or waded in knee-deep to watch her, fearing for her life since the day I heard her say to her mother, laughing and shivering as she towelled herself off, 'That water would stop your heart.'

Around the time that I was entering adolescence my grandparents came less and less often to the beach, until they no longer came at all. The slope was too treacherous for them. When I was sixteen, my grandfather died, and for the final two summers before I went off to college, the same year my grandmother sold the house and moved into a retirement home, it was just women on those visits, my mother and grandmother and me, and sometimes a girl-friend or two I'd brought along. We would sit round the fireplace at night, sororal and easy, but conscious, too, of the men who were not with us.

Years later, when my mother and Stan visited Eddie and me in Ireland after we were married, I took her to the beach at Rosses Point. It was early June, just the two of us. Stan had gone golfing with some men Eddie had introduced him to, and Eddie was working. As we descended the slope from the car park to the long second strand, my mother stopped and put her hand on my arm as though she had seen an apparition.

'What is it?' I said.

She took a deep breath and looked up and down the beach, surveying the horizon, then she put a hand to her chest and patted herself consolingly.

'Are you okay?'

'I'm fine,' she said, and for a moment said nothing more. When she had recovered herself, she told me that she had just experienced a sense of déjà vu so powerful she felt a bit unsteady. Something about the beach, she said, the precise elevation from which we were overlooking it, something about the weather, too, which was changing as we stood there. Just a minute ago, the sun had been out and it looked as though the day was going to get steadily brighter, but low, pewter clouds were now gathering above the water. She had felt transported, she said, right back to her parents' beach house, to that moment of approaching the top of the trail, before you descended through the trees, when you could see the beach and the sea spread before you.

'Do you remember that?' she said.

'Of course I do.'

We stood looking out over the strand until the thing that had come upon her seemed to pass and I felt her beside me again, in the here and now. As we started down the path, I hooked my arm through hers.

'Don't lose me,' she said. It was an old phrase of mine from childhood.

'Don't worry,' I said, and steered us towards the water. 'Let's put our toes in.'

At the water's edge we took off our shoes. A warm wind was blowing. Across the inlet, we could see the shoreline at Lissadell, and to the north the mountain behind our house. I traced an arc through the water with my foot and said, 'The cold would stop your heart.'

'It's not so bad,' my mother said, and I knew that she didn't remember. I told her then how I had lived in terror of her heart stopping whenever she was in the ocean, and instead of laughing she looked genuinely distraught. 'Why didn't you tell me?' she said. 'I don't know,' I said. And I didn't. There are many things like that in childhood, fears that could easily be allayed but which, in the overly literal realm we inhabit as children, make too much sense to question. It wasn't hard to believe that the icy water that sent needles of pain up my calves might also be sending similar, and deadly, shards into my mother's heart.

During the last year of her life, when we went to the beach near her condo she wouldn't go in the water. The Gulf was calm, but she didn't trust her balance. She said if she fell she would not be able to get up. Once, she let me lead her. I held her arm and we stood in water not even to our knees, and she looked happy, but then a small wave lapped against our shins and she tottered slightly and said, 'Whoa.' After that, she demurred whenever I asked her to come in with me, and while I swam in the calm shallows she sat under the beach umbrella, watching me so anxiously I felt I was torturing her.

Once, not long into the affair, Eddie and I were in the car when I heard Cauley's voice on the radio. I had a moment of dissociation, in which I was not sure if the voice was in my head – I often imagined what Cauley might say to me about this or that – followed by another moment in which I wondered, ridiculously, whether he might say something that would give us away.

We were coming home from Eddie's parents' house. Celia and Gerry had had their first baby three weeks before, Ethan was his name, and they had driven down to Sligo to show him off. We'd walked into the sitting room and Celia was in a big armchair, holding him. Gerry and Eddie's mother were bent over, eyeing the baby rapturously, and Eddie's father was to the left, leaning forward in his wheelchair. Everyone was silent, struck dumb by the miracle of Ethan blinking.

'Ah, come in!' Celia said when she saw us. 'The little guy is dying to meet you.'

She handed the baby to Eddie, who took him and rocked him gently, with a naturalness that surprised me. When he turned and offered Ethan to me, I panicked. I felt suddenly frail and shaky, the sort of person you wouldn't hand a baby to in a million years. But I couldn't possibly refuse, so I took him, and everyone looked on with their beatific smiles. The impulse to drop the infant was strong – I don't mean I wanted to, of course, but it was one of those unbidden urges, like veering into oncoming traffic or pitching yourself off a mountain path. Some part of me wanted to drop the baby and just come clean, because it was too much, the way they were all smiling at me, the way they'd entrusted me with this baby of theirs, as though I were someone who could be trusted with anything at all.

'Isn't that Kevin's pal?' Eddie said, as we turned up the mountain road. The show's host had just mentioned the names of his guests, Cauley and two others, who were there to discuss the future of the Abbey Theatre. 'The one you met in Dublin that time?'

I had told Eddie I was meeting Cauley for coffee before going to the hospital to interview the psychologist. The idea had been to carve out a plausible space in my life for Cauley to inhabit, though I could see now it would've been smarter to say nothing.

I pretended I hadn't been listening. 'Oh,' I said vaguely, and looked down at the radio. 'You're right, it is.'

'Did you ever hear back from him? Wasn't he going to set you up with some contacts?'

'No,' I said. 'I never heard back from him.'

Eddie gave a little snort. He had a particularly low opinion of people who made a show of saying they'd do this and that for you and then didn't deliver.

'I should've followed up,' I said. 'I didn't follow up.'

We listened for a minute. Then Eddie said, 'He sounds full of himself.'

Cauley went on and on. I felt an intimacy with him that was making me queasy. I had to resist the urge to turn the radio off. It was unbearable, Cauley's voice filling the car as though he were in it, and Eddie trying to talk to me about him, and me thinking: *How could he not know, how could he possibly not know?*

I reached over to turn the volume down, and my hand was shaking.

We met maybe a dozen times in all, when Eddie was travelling, or if I managed to secure some freelance assignment that took me to Dublin. A few times, I simply lied. I was meeting an old college friend who was passing through, or an editor I hoped to work for. Or I was researching some vague story idea. On every one of those occasions, when I left our home I imagined that when I returned all would be changed. Whatever vague intimations Eddie was feeling would crystallize, and he would grasp the truth. I thought that only in my absence could Eddie see me clearly, and each time I set out for Dublin, eager as I was for Cauley, I had to resist the urge to turn back.

And yet, once I was there, I found it hard to drag myself away. Soon Cauley was having to persuade me to hurry to the train station, for my own good; I was losing track of what was and wasn't prudent. Once, we argued over whether or not I should accompany him to the Abbey. It was an opening night, and he was reviewing the play. There would be a lot of people there he knew, and apart from the occasional drink in Dublin we didn't do public outings together. I had told him the day before that I would see him at the flat after the play. I actually relished the idea of hanging around Cauley's place on my own. I imagined myself stretched out on his bed, awaiting his return, feeling kept and illicit.

But when I got to Dublin that afternoon, we immediately made love, and as we lay there afterwards, playful and sated, feeding forkfuls of left-over Bolognese to each other from a bowl on the bed between us, I decided that I wanted to go to the Abbey after all.

I said, 'We could easily be friends, you know. It's not like it's the fifties.'

Cauley leaned across me to put the bowl on the floor and said, 'I thought we agreed it wasn't a good idea.'

'Someone there you don't want me to see?'

He propped himself up on one elbow and ran a finger down the length of my chest and belly. 'I'm not going to dignify that with a response.'

'That sounds like something my mother would say.'

He smiled. 'Well, you've always spoken well of your mother.'

'I'm serious,' I said.

'I want you to come, it would be lovely. But we decided against it for a good reason.'

I continued to protest. I felt a desire to be reckless, and yet I wasn't sure I wanted to win the argument. I wanted it both ways – for our secret to be protected, and for us to be seen together. In the end, I convinced him to bring me to the theatre. We readied ourselves in the flat, dressing and primping and sharing an iceless G&T. The normalcy of it thrilled me.

At the theatre, we had a drink in the lobby before the play

started, and anyone Cauley knew he introduced me to as a journalist, and he looked at me whenever I spoke with the sort of studied attention we direct at people in whom we are only politely interested. It was only in the theatre, when the lights went down, that he touched me, took my hand and placed it on the inside of his thigh, and whispered in my ear that he wanted to be home and fucking me.

The following day, as though alarmed by what we'd done, we didn't leave the flat. We ordered a Chinese and lay in bed watching *GoodFellas* on video, and Cauley told me about the time he went to New York. He was nineteen and had gone to stay with a cousin in Queens, thinking he might never come back. He was going to melt into the crowd and live by his wits and make his way in the theatre. His eyes got that glazed, far-away look I saw in even the most sophisticated, the most jaded, of Irish people when they talked about New York.

'I loved it,' he said, 'I loved New York.' But then his cousin's lease was up and the landlord was going to gut the place. Cauley's cousin moved in with his girlfriend, and Cauley bunked for several weeks with some bricklayers from Clare, tended bar and, over one sweltering summer, whittled his savings down to nothing and met no one at all from the theatre world.

'I came back with seven quid in my pocket,' he said, then smiled. 'But I'd lost weight.'

'I can't believe you never told me this,' I said.

'I wanted it all to happen fast, and when it didn't I lost my nerve. It embarrasses me, actually, how quickly I gave up.'

'Well,' I said. 'You'll go back.'

He didn't answer. He stared at the ceiling like someone whose one good shot was behind him. I nudged him with my knee and he turned to me and kissed me hard, his teeth on my lip, his hand reaching around my lower back to press me to him.

I had a ticket for the evening train. It was nearly five o'clock, the sun coming in full across the bed, the air swampy with heat and the sweat of us, and all I could do was lie there. I felt thick as syrup. I knew that if I didn't go a cascade of consequences would follow, but just then I was incapable of caring. I was like someone with heat stroke or hypothermia, the life-saving thing in view and unable to rouse myself to reach for it.

Cauley said, for the third time, 'You have to get up, sweetheart, you're going to miss your train.'

'I know,' I said, and I was grateful to him for keeping us on track, but only momentarily, for in the next instant I thought: Why was he so keen for me to leave? Where was he going? With whom? Sometimes he seemed so sad in his life, waiting there for me like a child. Other times I imagined that the minute I left him he opened the closet door and a party poured out.

Between encounters, we wrote letters to each other. It seems extravagant now, the exchange of letters, as though we had the leisure of aristocrats. I say *Cauley wrote me letters*, and it sounds like an affectation, like he was showing off. But it was just what people did then. What a commitment it seems now! The gathering of all that gear – the pen, the stationery, the envelope; the copying out of the address and the licking of the stamp; and then the effort of filling all those pages, the laborious scrawling that sends twinges up my wrist even to contemplate. But we had no choice. Phones were a problem. Cauley didn't have his own, just a pay phone in the hallway outside his bedsit. The age of the mobile had not properly dawned, and none of us had email yet. The first of the two times Cauley phoned the house, a few weeks into the affair, Eddie was right there. It was midday, a time when Eddie was never home. I answered, then constricted with fear at the sound of Cauley's voice, which seemed to rise an octave and go thin, now heart-rendingly unsure of itself – for he had heard the hesitation in my own voice. I spoke a few stilted non sequiturs that must've sounded ridiculous even to Eddie and cut the conversation short, and if there was a moment I felt most strongly the cheap, diminishing effect of adultery, it was that one.

The post arrived in the late morning, when Eddie was gone to work and the breakfast things were put away and the day yawned like some other life I could tumble into. It was the first true summer in six years, the first since the year of my arrival, though the heat and the light seemed in a different key entirely. It should've been an idyll – the laburnum coming into its own and the glen bathed in sunshine and Eddie and I languorous as honeymooners, enjoying perhaps our last summer unencumbered by children. Instead it felt infernal, the buzz-saw drone of insects wrongly loud. The light seemed wrong, too – sharp and hard, like light in the desert. By midday, the road to our house would be blistering in the heat.

Every day, I thought of my first summer with Eddie, the soft, purple-grey skies of midnight and the clarity with which he loved me. I had begun to believe that I had fallen in love with Eddie in part because of the way that he loved me. But if so, was that wrong? I still don't know. Because in loving him for that I was loving his capaciousness, his ability to accept me as I was, his refusal to be discouraged by my shortcomings or inconsistencies in my character. He was like an *example* of love, and I envied him his certainty. I thought it might rub off on me. Nothing I had done, or ever might do, seemed to alarm him. And nothing was required of me in the way of change. It was the antidote to the feeling that had nagged at me since childhood, instilled in me by my father's absence – the feeling that true home was elsewhere, off in the mythical distance, the belief that if things were going to come right, some change was required of me, the nature of which was maddeningly obscure.

Each morning, when Eddie's car disappeared down the laneway, I felt a shameful relief, and then the anticipation would begin. Around eleven a letter would come, or it wouldn't come. If there was nothing, I felt safe leaving the house and getting on with my day. If a letter did arrive, I would sit on the front steps, the wave of a mountain breaking behind me and the bay glistening in the distance in front and the garden awash in sunlight – a light that seemed no longer accusatory or even familiar but like an element from another realm entirely. I would hold the envelope unopened for as long as I could bear, my hands trembling with excitement but also with the previous night's excesses, for Eddie and I had no idea how to hide from ourselves that summer and so fell back on the things we knew: the late nights and the revelry of our beginnings, which in their first instance had had the feel of celebration but which we now relived as bad theatre.

Inside on Eddie's desk was one of those shiny letter openers, but out of some flimsy notion of honour I never used it, instead hooking my index finger in the little gap at one end of the envelope and running it to the opposite end, producing a ragged furrow that looked like agony itself. I can still see Cauley's handwriting, schoolboyish and deliberate, which contrasted sharply with the prose, a torrent of ideas and sentiments that seemed to contain all the energy of his person. Each letter was a welter of allusions – to public things, things between the two of us, things meaningful only to himself. It was part of what drew me to him. I wanted to gather him in, to get at whatever was underneath the performance, under all that exclamatory bonhomie. I wanted to see him weep – not over me, but over the past, his parents, life, whatever he'd failed at or feared, the whole sad, fucked-up story. I wanted to see him grow small and helpless and racked with suffering, and then to gather that suffering up and rock it like a baby. What is it with women, our way of looking at men like they are prisoners we've been tasked to break?

I suppose it should embarrass me now, to remember the hours that summer that I whiled away just thinking of him, drifting idly about the house, wallowing in love as though it were indeed my whole existence, its interior labours actual demands upon my time. But it doesn't embarrass me, not as much as other things I did. In fact, I feel astonished, and a tad nostalgic, to recall the frittering away of entire days.

Did I believe we had a future? I honestly can't remember. I remember the way he made his As, squat and nearly square, but I cannot recall whether I actually thought it might work between us, what I wished for, or thought possible. I lived in the now, as though the affair were a terrible crisis in which the intensity of the present and its demands simply effaced, for some necessary interval, any consideration of the future. But I must've thought about it. I must've thought about little else that summer.

It is just after ten when we step outside the cinema on Eustace Street. A desultory bit of snow catches us both by surprise.

'Oh?' we say, looking up.

'What's this?' Harry says, smiling at me, delighted. It is perhaps my favourite thing about Harry, that quick access to delight. He looks as though he has never seen anything quite so magical as these few aimless flurries drifting down upon Temple Bar on a night in March.

We didn't go to the cinema together, and it was only half-way through the film that I noticed him, two rows in front of me and over on the far left, alone. He was utterly engrossed, his head tilted back slightly, his face catching the glow of the screen, and in the dark, in the intimacy of the cinema, I felt I was spying him in a private moment. Afterwards, I waited for him in the lobby, and when he saw me he lifted his eyebrows in greeting and gave me a reluctant little smile. There was something sad and subdued about him, and I thought maybe I'd been wrong to wait.

The film was about a couple in their eighties who'd been together for ever. They lived in an apartment in Paris. One day, the woman suffered a stroke. The prognosis was that she could expect more strokes, a rapid deterioration in her mental and physical condition. She made her husband promise he wouldn't leave her in a hospital to die. As the weeks and months passed, she grew more disabled, more demented. She lay on the bed in her nightdress, and her husband exercised her leg: *neuf, dix, onze, douze* . . . The nightdress slipped to reveal the skin of her thigh, mottled and unsightly. In another scene, he watched her being showered by a nurse. Her slack breasts, the folds of her belly. There was no aversion in him, simply the frank gaze of a lifetime. At the film's end, when his wife was capable of little but lying on the bed and moaning *hurts* . . . over and over, he suffocated her with a pillow, in a terrible act of mercy.

Harry and I decide to walk up to the Central Hotel for a drink. I scoot round to the right side of him, the side opposite his walking stick. His bad leg seems not to belong to him, like a slightly awkward bundle he is toting. It turned out I was wrong about it being polio. It was a botched back operation when he was in his early thirties that was meant to deal with some damage to his discs. Afterwards, they told him he'd never walk again.

'Irish health care in the eighties,' he said. 'You don't want to know.'

He'd spent six months in a wheelchair, then nursed himself – his neurons – back to some kind of working order. He said he'd stand by the fireplace, clutching the mantel with one hand, timing himself with a stopwatch. Ten seconds today, twelve tomorrow, and so on, until he was able to stand with just the walking stick, and then to walk.

'Does it hurt?' I asked him recently. 'Your leg.'

'And my back.' He said he gets shooting pains down the right side of his body, sometimes down his arm. His knee is bad. 'There are places it's nearly bone on bone.'

We find an empty sofa in the hotel bar and order two glasses of red wine. 'Well,' he says brightly, 'what did you think?' He has recovered himself. He no longer looks caught out and is ready to discuss the film's artistic merits.

'It was a proper love story,' I say. 'He did the worst thing, the last thing he could ever have imagined doing, because she'd asked him to. Did you like it?'

'It was unrelenting. I liked it very much.'

We agree: watching the film was like watching death slowly bearing down on you. There was something beautifully, horribly, true about it.

'They won't like it in America,' Harry says, a bit gleefully. Another thing Harry enjoys: the gormless, adolescent optimism of America. Harry is an old soul, European through and through.

'No,' I say. 'Probably not.'

He looks to his left, he's caught sight of someone he recognizes. And just like that I remember: Harry, standing in front of the shell of a burnt-out house.

'Hey,' I say. 'I remember. The assessment in Kosovo. I remember meeting you.'

Harry turns back to me. 'Don't try to flatter me,' he jokes. 'It's too late.'

'I do,' I say. 'I'm serious. I'm sorry it took me so long. I don't think we really spoke.'

'We were introduced,' he says. 'They had just killed a bunch of dogs in the next village. Do you remember that?'

I have to think for a minute. 'Yes,' I say, 'vaguely.' I had a way, back then, of forgetting things that didn't make it into my reports. My memory became weirdly utilitarian. My entire relationship to events grew strange, in fact. When I'd first arrived in Kosovo, I had wanted to imbue my reports with feeling – outrage or sorrow – which was exactly what I was not supposed to do. In Sri Lanka, I had written a lot of human-interest stories: people getting new limbs, the displaced being resettled, grass-roots peace activists running community centres. My job was to make donors feel good about what their money had achieved. So although I never lied, I focused on the positive. Every life could have a new beginning. War was not all. Hope springs eternal.

But in Kosovo I was writing for internal consumption. My job was to stand apart from the thicket of propaganda and hysteria, to record barbarity – a murder, a mass grave, a firebombed church, a whole village expelled – with the same detachment I brought to an update on the electricity supply. I took to these communiqués with an ease that surprised me. I understood the authority of dispassion, and felt strangely at home in it.

'The dogs had rabies,' I say. 'Wasn't that the story?'

'That was the story,' Harry says. 'But killing the dogs was a warning. The village was being cleared.'

'Awful we should've met over a bunch of murdered dogs.'

'When I think of Kosovo,' Harry says, 'I think of dogs. Dogs, everywhere.'

'I know,' I say. 'I know what you mean.'

The dogs in Priština were all skinny as greyhounds, and they slithered along the dark streets in threes or fours, burying their snouts in the waist-high piles of stinking rubbish, snorting and sneezing, gnawing at God knows what. Those that weren't wild were kept chained by the neck in the yards of their owners, where they barked and bayed all through the night. When you passed they would leap forward with shocking vigour, before their chains yanked them back to earth. All that animal energy, grown twisted and violent from having for so long been denied any normal outlet.

I had a dog of my own, a stray little mongrel who'd attached herself to me. I named her Betty. She had such a relentlessly happy disposition that she seemed a bit stupid. One day when my friend Stephen was visiting, we took Betty to be spayed, which, in the context of Kosovo, where strays were shot or left to fend for themselves, seemed an act of pointless or excessive care. Stephen was Welsh. We had met in Sri Lanka. Around the time I went to Kosovo, he went to Juba in South Sudan. After that we'd see each other three or four times a year. Either he came to visit me or we met in some more pleasant location – the Dalmatian coast or the Mediterranean. We were comfortable together, not heated or tortured, just good. I respected Stephen, respected his self-sufficiency. He could repair an engine and build a shelter out of nothing, and navigate by dead reckoning. He was like an explorer from the nineteenth century, someone most himself when alone. He'd go off on long solo safaris or extended cross-country ski treks. But the relationship lacked traction, it didn't have a trajectory; we were as close or as far from each other after three years as we'd been after a few months. Anyway, his plan was eventually to retire from this work and take up the family farm in Wales, and I had no desire to end up on a farm in Wales, with Stephen or anyone else. Still, I felt envious. I envied the way he inhabited his life. I thought he knew himself, utterly.

The vet was an Albanian from Tirana, his name was Bekim. He worked for the Department of Veterinary Services, and he told us we should come only after 6 p.m., which meant that he was pocketing the money. We arrived at 6.15. On the wall of Bekim's office were pictures of a horse, a parrot, a rabbit and a goat, all made of a cheap velvet material, and a poster showing an American flag.

I told Bekim I wanted to watch the procedure, and he looked at me with interest and scepticism. He gave Betty a shot and a few minutes later slit her open like an envelope and began pulling what looked like a long tongue out of her. Then he stopped, cursed and tucked the tongue back into her, the way you'd tuck a tissue up your sleeve. I had no idea how things were meant to be unfolding, but this didn't look right. There was a lot of blood – dark, thick, purply-red – pooling on the table. I looked at Stephen. He raised his eyebrows but didn't say anything.

After some more rummaging around, Bekim extracted something glistening and stringy with his tongs. He started across the room with it towards the garbage can but then looked at me and stopped and, instead, dropped it at his feet on the floor, as though issuing a challenge. The floor was already smeared with blood, and he was now operating with the dog's long, stringy bits at his feet. I was afraid he was going to slip or, worse, that he would step on them and blood and other liquids would squirt out.

Finally, he sewed up Betty's insides and stitched her skin, then he stooped and picked up the stringy thing and laid it on the table. He pointed out the uterus. I looked at Betty. She was comatose, defenceless. I thought I had never seen a being more innocent. Bekim poked her gently in the face a few times with his finger and said, 'She is taking the medicine a little too seriously.'

'You didn't kill her,' I said, half joking.

Bekim didn't answer, either because my question was absurd or because he considered the dog's death of negligible import. He motioned for Stephen to lift her off the table. I put an old blanket under her and Stephen lowered her on to it and carried her to the car, then he set her gently on the back seat. As we drove away in silence I had the sense that we had shared in something elemental, a ritual of bloodletting.

Harry asks me if I read about the horse and cattle carcasses that were found at the bottom of a cliff in Doonbeg last week. I did. Their ears had been cut off to remove identifying tags and then they'd been pitched three hundred feet from the clifftop. There were tyre marks up to the edge of the cliff. The vet who examined them – there were sixteen dead animals – said it had been hard to count them, because their necks and legs were broken and their limbs were all tangled together and they were rotting. He said it was the worst job he'd ever had to do.

We sit there gloomily, in silence. Then Harry says that the difference between nations is the degree to which acts of everyday barbarity are tucked away, conducted out of sight, and that what we call civilization, and what we know as peace, is only the papering over of what we really are: violent, venal, full of fear.

There was a programme on TV the other night that we both saw. It was about the sex trade in Ireland, now divided into outdoor prostitution, which sounds hale and vigorous but just means standing on street corners, and indoor prostitution, which sounds cosy but means the women have been trafficked from Eastern Europe and Nigeria and are hustled from county to county, from brothel to brothel. There was CCTV footage of a few of them in a car park in Athlone, with their little wheelie suitcases and their cheap trainers, scurrying behind their pimp like dogs he was walking but didn't much like.

Harry says that if the nation were a rock we could lift we'd be horrified by what we saw. The two of us are essentially in agreement on this: that human beings have an infinite capacity for cruelty. I say to him, 'I wish it were a happier world view we shared.'

'I believe goodness exists,' he says. 'And love. You do, too. You loved your mother. And you've loved other people. Isn't that a world view?'

'I don't know. I suppose.'

'Of course it is.'

We order another glass of wine each.

'I met an old friend of Eddie's today,' I say.

Harry's eyes go wide. He knows that I was married, but nothing at all about the break-up. 'Really? Where?'

'On Wicklow Street.'

He sips his wine. 'And how was that?'

'Strange,' I say. 'I never liked the guy. But it was one of those times where you stop to say hello because you're sure you know the person from somewhere, and by the time you realize who he is and where you know him from and that you'd rather not talk to him it's too late.'

'So you spoke to him?'

'Briefly. I asked about Eddie.'

'And?'

'He didn't say much. He did tell me Eddie'd sold the house. The one we lived in. I asked him where Eddie was living now and he just said he was still in the area. With his family.'

Harry can see the encounter has thrown me, though he doesn't know why, and I'm not sure myself.

'Why did he sell the house?' Harry asks.

'No idea,' I say. 'I didn't want to ask.' I resented hearing about Eddie from this particular man, who I sensed was enjoying my discomfort, and I didn't want to give him the satisfaction of my curiosity. I was surprised at the twinge of possessiveness I felt. I had known, of course, that the house was for sale, but I hadn't anticipated that Eddie's leaving it would have any particular effect on me, that I would be unsettled by the fact that, suddenly, I had no idea where to picture him.

Harry keeps eyeing me but doesn't comment. He is doing that thing men sometimes do. You tell them something big and confusing, something that's really rocked you, the sort of thing that would make a woman scoot forward on her chair so that the two of you could parse the thing to death, and they say nothing. And you are never sure if they are holding it there, in silence and respect, letting you sort it the way they sort things, or if they are simply at a loss, unable to cross easily from the territory of information to the territory of feeling.

By the time we leave the Central, it has stopped snowing and doesn't even feel terribly cold. We walk together down to the corner of Dame Street, where the twenty-four-hour Spar is, with its plate-glass windows that glare like a huge television. Harry kisses me, once on each cheek, and says, as always, 'Mind yourself.' And, as always, after a few steps, I turn to watch him go. I worry about him in the city, at night. Not just that he couldn't run if he had to – does anyone really run from muggers? – but that with all the drunkenness and the jostling, he might be knocked to the ground. I'm making him sound old, or enfeebled, and he is neither, but it can be bedlam in this little knot of streets at night.

When I get back to Monkstown, I go straight to the laptop and type in the address of Eddie's house, our old house. Sure enough, the place has sold. I go from website to website, everywhere it was listed, but the photos of the interior have been removed. A jolt passes through me, a kick of panic, as though someone has padlocked a place I'd half considered mine.

It was midsummer before I told anyone about Cauley. Camille had gone back to Toronto the previous autumn, and I saw less of Jane since Eddie and I had moved out of the town. Cauley had told Kevin, and this made me nervous. Once, when Eddie and I were in Mulligan's having a rare drink in town, we bumped into Kevin. He was on his way to being drunk, and I kept catching him staring at me.

'What did he say when you told him?' I'd asked Cauley.

'He said that Eddie was a sound guy.' Cauley looked almost sad.

'Nice,' I said. A lot of people – men, actually – said that about Eddie. It reminded me that Eddie had another world, the world of men, with its own clear codes and criteria. 'So does that mean his loyalties are divided?'

'Don't worry,' Cauley said. 'We're friends since we were six.'

The next time I met Kevin on the street it was like meeting my gynaecologist, a relative stranger who possessed knowledge of my most intimate life.

I had no confidant of my own. Kevin was Cauley's friend, and I resisted the temptation to unburden myself to him, to enjoy an hour devoid of duplicity. There were days when it felt as though my very thoughts were in knots, and there were other times I experienced a clear-headedness that brooked no doubt. But I was afraid this clarity was itself a delusion, an indication of how far from reality I had strayed.

Was Cauley only playing? Was I? And if we were, would we even know it?

I had read an article recently about what people do when they get lost – in a city, or when driving, or walking in a wilderness. There are identifiable stages, like the stages of grief, and, not surprisingly, the first is denial. That's when we 'bend the map', try to force the features we see before us to align with those indicated on a map, even though the correspondence between them is obviously poor. We focus on details that seem to confirm what we already believe to be true and ignore evidence to the contrary. I thought, as I read, that this sort of 'reasoning' was hardly confined to being lost and in fact probably directed the bulk of our life's decision-making. The more distinctive stages come when denial breaks down, when we can no longer pretend that we aren't lost. Adrenalin surges, panic sets in. Our perceptions become distorted. When this happens, the article said, it is best to 'stay put and engage in a quiet activity to calm the mind', which is – do I need to say it? – the very last thing we are likely to do. Instead, we will choose from a handful of strategies, including 'backtracking', 'route sampling' and 'view enhancing', deceptively rational-sounding terms for actions undertaken in alarm. The funny thing is that lost people – despite the fact that they often wander considerably long distances in their panicked peregrinations – are likely to be found relatively close to their last-known position. In other words, they could just as profitably have stayed put and engaged in a quiet activity to calm the mind.

The article had a short but terrifying sidebar on spatial

disorientation among pilots, a condition in which perceptions no longer agree with reality. In order to give his non-pilot readers a point of reference, the writer began by referring to the common experience of sitting in a stationary train when an adjacent train begins to pull away, creating the sensation that we are moving backwards. He then went on to describe the myriad reasons pilots become disoriented: non-visible or false horizons, night flying over featureless terrain, the strange things manoeuvres such as turning, banking, levelling and climbing do to our vestibular system. There is a whole dark vocabulary of disorientation: the 'leans', the 'black-hole approach illusion', the 'graveyard spiral'. Many fatal accidents in private planes are the result of pilots lacking the training to fly with reference to instruments or, out of inexperience or panic, trusting their perceptions over what the instrumentation is telling them.

Upon finishing the article, I thought two things: that the key to being a successful liar was the ability to keep your nerve when your mind was playing tricks on you, and that the affair I was having might merely be a futile detour I was taking within my marriage and in the end I would wind up not the far side of anything but right back where I'd started — with Eddie.

I was in town when I bumped into Jane. I had come to turn in a piece I'd done for the local paper on the current state of a twenty-year-long battle over a proposed relief road through town (this was the tail end of the old days, when things still happened in three dimensions, and I trudged into the office and handed them four typed pages), and I was headed to the phone box to ring Eddie, who I'd been trying to reach for the last three hours. I'd worked myself into a state of anxiety, convinced – not for the first time – that Eddie had found out everything and needing desperately to hear his voice, to be reassured he hadn't. It was a terribly cheap feeling, and the relief that followed each time I got my reassurance was so great that it left me vowing, for a few hours, to forsake Cauley.

I saw Jane on the opposite corner of Wine Street. She spotted me at almost the same instant. She smiled, and then an odd look crossed her face and she signalled that I should wait and she would cross to my side. By the time she reached me, I was feeling the full wallop of a panic attack. Jane's voice sounded to me like it was coming from inside my own head. I looked down at the footpath, which quivered slightly, as though it might crawl away.

'Are you okay?' she said.

I don't know how people know what to do, how they know to just take you in hand and talk to you until it passes. But that's what Jane did. We stood on the street and she stroked me like you would a cat, and after a minute or two I stopped shaking. She had a little place on Harmony Hill, and we went there and sat at her kitchen table and I told her everything, or almost everything. She listened very carefully, and when finally I paused she said that she was incredibly sorry to hear all this but that, to be honest, she wasn't shocked.

I looked at her. There is nothing to make you feel foolish like someone telling you that your greatest secret is hardly a surprise.

'I remember the day you got married,' she said. 'I was thinking what a strange thing love is – I mean, strange like miraculous – because it allows two very different people to see things in each other that aren't so apparent to anyone else.'

'You mean you thought it was far-fetched?'

'No. I thought the two of you were very different, that's all. When I say I'm not surprised, I don't mean I didn't think it could work. You know,' she said, 'I've always thought he loved you. Any time I've seen you together, that's what I thought.'

I stayed at Jane's for a few hours. She cooked a stir-fry and we talked about her job testing water up and down the west coast, and then about a guy from Derry she'd been seeing. He was doing a Ph.D. in environmental toxicology and had just come back from field work in Indonesia. She showed me a photo of him. He had a beard and was standing on a beach, in wet-weather gear and a woolly hat, and he was smiling. He looked like one of those men who are instinctively at home in the elements. Her life seemed astonishingly *clean* to me, simple in the best sense, and my own, in comparison, seedy and scrambled.

I put the picture down very carefully on the table and told Jane that I was happy for her.

'What are you going to do?' she said, as though she hadn't heard me.

I shook my head. 'I don't know.'

The following day was Saturday. As Eddie and I puttered around the kitchen making coffee, he told me about a dream he'd had the night before. In the dream, he had jumped off a cliff – or perhaps he'd been pushed, he couldn't be sure – and he was flying, or floating, through the air, down, down, down, a little nervous but mostly curious. Then, abruptly, he realized that he would never hit the ground, and he became more rather than less afraid. The thought that he would keep falling through space, for ever – that that was *his* eternity – horrified him. He said it was the most frightening dream he'd had in ages.

I bent to pour some Kibbles into Olivia's bowl and didn't look at him. I thought: he wants me to go, he feels us in a limbo that is worse than the worst resolution. I have become a burden. I have become, literally, a nightmare.

A week later, I tried to leave him. I didn't say that I was leaving him. I told him I was going to Jane's for the night. I said a few of us were having dinner and there'd be lots of wine and I'd be better staying over. What I intended was to drive all the way to Dublin, check into a hotel and call Eddie from there in the morning, to tell him it was over. It was cowardly, but I reasoned that the amount of pain inflicted would, in the end, be hardly more than if I'd sat him down in our front room for the announcement. I hadn't told Cauley either. Only after I'd phoned Eddie would I go to Cauley's bedsit and reveal what I had done. In a strange way, all these convolutions and half-truths thrilled me. I felt as though I were finally taking hold of matters, making firm decisions.

I hadn't allowed myself to think much beyond the moment of my arrival at Cauley's, but I was in thrall to my vision of that moment, the intensity of feeling that would follow my delivering myself to Cauley, the place it would assume in our mythology. Any uncertainties about how Cauley would receive me, now that I was all his, were masked by my excitement. What I had managed to make myself believe was that, once the deed was done, whatever doubts Cauley might have would evaporate; there would be only our future to embark on.

I packed an overnight bag, just some essentials to get me through a few days. I'd have to come back for my things, of course, but that could be accomplished once the news had sunk in with Eddie. I seemed to have assumed that the practicalities of separating would be neatly split from the emotional storm, that there would be a linear progression of foreseeable phases and that we would proceed through them with rationality and order.

Around eight, I kissed Eddie goodbye in the front hall and set off. As I descended the mountain road, faster than was wise, I felt as though the car might rise from the earth and become airborne. I was that giddy. I had to force myself to slow down.

It was only when I was the far side of town that it began to dawn on me what I was doing. By the time I'd passed through Carrick-on-Shannon, I was asking myself if I really needed to go all the way to Dublin to accomplish my mission. Dublin seemed very far away, a point of no return. Perhaps I should carry on only as far as Longford. Then I thought of waking up in Longford, and it seemed no way to begin the rest of my life. I was some miles beyond Dromod when my heart began to race. I wanted to pull over but wasn't sure I should risk it on the shoulder or how exactly to execute the move – I was travelling, along with everybody else, at about 100 kilometres per hour. In the space of an instant, I grew terrified of the fact of myself behind the wheel of a fast-moving car, and I thought if I didn't get off that road immediately I was going to lose control completely. A petrol station appeared, and I swerved into the forecourt and switched off the engine, breathless and drained of all bravado.

I sat there for probably half an hour, the windows open to the warm night, a homely rhythm to the scene – the comings and goings of cars to the petrol pumps, people in and out of the shop for cigarettes or sweets or a pint of milk, the faces of children, sleepy and dumbstruck, in car windows. The shaking in my hands eased, my heartbeat slowed to normal. There was a sense of relief in discovering I hadn't the courage to go through with it.

I thought of phoning Eddie. There was a phone box outside the little shop. I heard myself telling him that I was coming home, the good news, as though I'd been given the all-clear after a health scare. The feeling, or some variation on it, was familiar. I'd felt it every time I came home after being with Cauley: how close I'd come to peril and ruin, and how thrilling, suddenly, the safety of the hearth. Each time, in his innocence, Eddie looked precious to me all over again and I was abject with tenderness.

I started the car and pulled out of the petrol station, and headed west, towards home. I stuck to the speed limit and cars zoomed by me, driven by people who seemed frighteningly sure of themselves.

When I pulled into our driveway it was almost midnight, the mountain behind the house huge and implacable. The moon was nearly full, and a few clouds floated by, mercury-coloured in the moonlight. I went round to the kitchen door, so as not to wake Eddie, along the path that ran beside the big back garden. We'd done nothing with the plans we'd drawn up for it that spring, and it was even wilder now and more overgrown than it had been the day we'd bought the house. It had assumed an aura of the unapproachable, a monument to our mysterious inertia, and I sometimes imagined it growing and spreading until it engulfed the house itself.

Eddie was in bed. I put my bag down at the foot of the stairs and went into the living room. I pulled the curtain and opened the sliding glass door, and moonlight spilled like smoke into the room. The front garden looked impossibly still. It was a small rockery, everything in it diminutive: the baby strawberries, dwarf heather that looked like bonsai shrubs, tiny purple-petalled flowers squeezing through the crevices. If the back garden was a jungle, there was a tension about the front; it was all control, tightness, denial. I thought of the woman who'd owned the house before us, the woman with anorexia. When we'd first moved in I used to imagine I could feel her here – she'd left a lot of herself behind, in the form of objects and decor but also an air of malaise that didn't lift until we'd stripped nearly every literal remnant of her existence away. Only the rockery served as a reminder.

Eventually, I climbed the stairs and got into bed. Eddie stirred but didn't wake, and I pressed against his broad back, feeling small and depleted.

The days after that were tentative and muted, as though we were awaiting news of some kind. I wasn't sleeping well. It felt more like jet lag than insomnia, abetted by the summer light. I never got used to the seasonal fluctuations at that latitude – the twenty-hour days of summer, going to bed when there was still light in the sky. I would crawl, exhausted, between the sheets at ten o'clock, then wake at three or four and lie there tossing, my mind as restless as if I were on stimulants, as the dawn bled blueish-white into the room. Around six I would fall again into a deep sleep, waking groggy and rueful, having slept, once again, through Eddie's dressing and departure.

One evening, after a hot, heavy rain, I said that I was going for a walk. It was about eight o'clock. There was an unusual light, lime-tinted, which was making everything – the trees and grass, the hedges, the one house opposite us – appear backlit and artificial, like pieces in a stage set. I wanted to be out in it, and away, for a few minutes, from Eddie. The following afternoon he was flying to the south of England on business, and I was heading to Dublin to be with Cauley for two whole days. As always, just before I saw Cauley, I was jangled, woozy with anticipation.

When I said I was going for a walk, Eddie said, 'I'll come.' My heart quickened. I nearly said, *Why?*

'Okay,' I said meekly. I opened the door and Olivia shot

out, looked in both directions with a twitch and headed off at a canter up the back garden.

When we were on the road Eddie took my hand and said, out of the blue, 'I was thinking maybe mid-September we might go to see your mother and Stan.'

'Really?' I took this in. 'You'd go, too?' My mother and Eddie loved each other, and he and Stan got on well, but usually Eddie was working and I went alone to Florida. I was aware I'd sounded uninviting, and added, 'Can you take holidays?'

'I should be able to.'

'That would be great,' I said, though what I felt was terror. Terror that, come September, none of this would exist; terror that my mother would never look at me in the same way again; terror – yes, this, too, occurred to me – that Eddie and my mother had spoken and decided I needed to get away and that some kind of intervention was on the cards. Perhaps Eddie meant to leave me there, return me to my mother, like merchandise that had not performed as promised.

Oh, I had so much shame that summer.

'We could rent a car,' he said, 'take them down to the Keys.'

'They'd love that,' I said, staring straight ahead at the dark bank of trees at the T-junction the far end of our road. 'She and Stan used to go to Key West. They haven't been in a while.'

'When were we there? Was it *four* years ago?'

'I think,' I said.

'Gas,' he said. 'Time flies.'

My jaw was clenched. I had begun to feel faint, and frighteningly insubstantial, as I had in the car the other night, as I had on the street corner the day I met Jane.

'I need to sit.' I rested on a stone wall bordering a neighbour's field.

Eddie stood looking at me. 'Y'all right?' he said, lightly, distractedly, as though he neither needed nor expected an answer.

When I swallowed, my throat felt swollen. 'I'm okay,' I said. 'I just got light-headed.'

He sat down beside me and put his arm around my lower back and gazed out towards the bay, which was half in cloud and half in a low sun. He said not another word. I could feel him sturdy beside me in that way of his, self-evident and unafraid. I tried to steady myself. I let my head rest on his shoulder and stared out at the view, that scoop of earth between the mountain and the bay, with its tufts of trees and its geometry of fields, the hay sheds and the new dormers and the dank little cottages.

The minutes passed. Colours came and went in the sky.

I thought maybe the time had come, that he was inviting me to come clean, and the temptation to do so was enormous. Maybe this was my chance and I should take it. Maybe there would be a worse price to pay if I didn't speak now. But I was too exhausted by secrecy, by the guilt and all the unwelcome power that came with it, to judge whether confessing was the wise thing to do, or whether now was the time.

I had begun to believe that Eddie knew something was going on, and knew it was in Dublin. When I'd returned from my last assignation with Cauley, he was in the sitting room reading the paper. It was about nine in the evening. I walked in, and he folded the paper on his lap and stared at me and didn't say hello.

'What's wrong?' I'd asked, because he looked a little shocked.

He shook his head, as though emerging from some preoccupation. 'Nothing,' he said, but clearly there was something. His tone, it seemed, was intended to suggest as much. The normal thing would be to press him – what *is* it? – but the last thing I wanted was an answer.

'Nothing,' he repeated. 'Welcome home.'

I'd spent the days after in a state of paranoia, certain Eddie was observing the signs of strain in me, waiting for me to crack, not wanting to ask me the question either – *what is it?* – because he didn't want to hear my answer.

'Let's go home,' I whispered, and we rose together and turned back down the lane.

It was only when we reached the house and Eddie asked me if I wanted tea that I was struck by the fact that he'd hardly seemed puzzled, or even surprised, by my spell of dizziness and incapacitation. True, he was one of those men who don't ask a lot of questions. In his case, it wasn't narcissism or self-importance but rather a notion of himself – was it even conscious? – as an anchor. His job was not to get caught up in passing storms or details but to stay solid and a bit apart. This was one of the things I had first loved about him, the steadiness with which he conducted himself. But that night I found it strange. Eddie was always the first to suggest I see the doctor for some minor ache or pain, and here I'd been faint for no reason and he hadn't even expressed curiosity, let alone concern. Still, for the rest of the evening he was exceptionally gentle, solicitous, even in his silence. He was like someone auditioning for the part of my husband.

Around eleven, he said he was heading up to bed. The announcement felt loaded. It was a night we might've made love, the mood was like that, an off-kilter intensity that seemed poised to tip towards the erotic. I felt he wanted to claim me, and I was surprised by a flush of desire. Something illicit seemed to course between us. I shifted on the sofa and thought of calling him over to me, having him right there, hungrily and fast. Then I thought of Cauley, and I couldn't do it.

'Goodnight,' I said. 'I'll be up later.'

He tossed a magazine on the chair and left the room.

I stayed up for a long time that night. I turned off the lamps and sat there in the dark, and a feeling of deadness came over me. I don't mean that I felt numb, but that I felt posthumous, as though I were surveying it all from on high, this life that no longer had anything to do with me. I thought of an evening some weeks before when I'd come home from Dublin. I had been with Cauley that day, I still smelled of him, and I'd sniffed at my own skin like an animal. On the days I'd been to his place, I felt sly and almost predatory afterwards, plugged into the world in a whole new way. It wasn't that the world had changed but that I was sensing more of its aspects. I looked at men differently, and they did the same to me. The air hummed with arousal, as though they knew what I'd been up to, and I felt initiated and vaguely criminal, on the other side of some line where I understood myself better and felt the worse for it. Back at home that evening I had sat on the brick step on the edge of the rockery, where the strawberry vines spread like tiny fingers in the dirt. The air was balmy and there was a wash of light from the west, a peach-coloured sun sinking below the firs that blocked our house from the road. I had wanted to get to the house before Eddie did. I'd felt the need to present myself to it, not quite to prostrate myself, but something not far from it. I'd wanted to walk into our home and feel forgiven, the way one feels when with animals or children, as though innocence were a contagious thing and reacquiring it as simple as being in its presence.

My mother loved sunsets. She considered them events. She liked to place herself at a certain beachside café near her condo and watch the sun disappear. Sometimes we did this when I visited her, though I had little interest in sunsets and, to my subsequent regret, often told her so. 'I don't get it,' I would say, 'why anyone would ever take a picture of a sunset. It's not like you capture anything of the splendour. It's not like it isn't going to happen again tomorrow.'

She would shake her head and smile wryly. 'You never know when the world will end.'

'Well, if it does,' I'd say, 'nobody's going to be looking at their photo albums.'

What was wrong with me, raining on her parade like that? My mother gazed at the horizon with a look of rapture, and I sat there parsing the experience for value.

One evening, not long after Stan's death, something in me shifted. We were sitting in our usual place, on high stools at the café, overlooking the beach and the Gulf. As the sun was sinking, a long, washed-out crimson band appeared above the line of the horizon, throbbing faintly like a heartbeat. As we watched, the colours appeared to intensify, as though the sun might flare and ignite. I glanced at my mother, who was watching it all with an air of beatific calm, so at home in the world, and still so capable of awe. I wondered how Stan's death had changed the tenor of such moments for her, whether these everyday majesties had intensified or been diminished. I looked back towards the horizon just in time to see a green flash as the sun vanished beyond the curve of the earth. My mother gasped, and I was speechless in the face of the sheer, soundless spectacle of the pulsing world.

After that, I tried to make a point of watching the sunset, even if only from the driver's seat of my car, to be mindful of the colours the sky assumed on any given evening. In Nairobi, I was often on my way home from work. It was always around half past six, that time of day when the heat seemed to draw, like a tide, back into itself. It became like a call to prayer, that hour, a time when I began, ritually, to think about my mother, minutes in which the whole of our history came to me in the form of a mood, as love is a mood, so that everything was coloured, briefly, by the knowledge of her existence.

Stan's death knocked her sideways, not just emotionally but mentally. She grew anxious and forgetful. She was overwhelmed by the smallest things. She became fixated on the +/− button on her old Nokia; she believed this was the key to keeping the device working. I told her, again and again, that this was only the volume control. She said that when she pushed the button she got a little green door. Yes, I said, the green bars are for volume. But now it's disappeared, she would say, sounding almost panicked. Yes, I would say, when it's not being adjusted, it won't stay on the screen. She was also obsessed with charging her phone. Though she very rarely used it, she became nervous if it was away from the charger for even an hour.

Throughout that period, which she mostly emerged

from – the confusion of grief lifted and she regained her equilibrium – I alternated between great frustration and the feeling of falling in love with her, over and over again. I felt a deep, almost unbearable pity for her humanity.

When she died, two years after Stan's death, I kept certain things, odd things I wouldn't have expected, including that flip-top phone. When I look at it I see her snapping it smartly shut, a misleading air of mastery, some trace remnant of the years when she was young and strong and sure of herself.

During her dying, which I mark as having begun in the late spring of last year with the sequence of mini-strokes, I used to think of hairline fractures spreading like veins across an ice sheet. Now, what I think of mostly is how small she got, how I could've lifted her and carried her, loose-boned and limp, as though from a battlefield.

One of the strokes happened when I was with her. We were pottering about the house, deciding whether to go to the beach or not, when she began to speak in a kind of mashed-up English. I looked at her, expecting her to right herself; occasionally, in playfulness, she made nonsense sounds, to indicate something hardly worth going into. *Yada yada yada*, she'd say, and roll her eyes. But this was different. She didn't seem to know it was happening. She stood before me, perfectly clear-eyed, perfectly steady, speaking gibberish. She was like a person possessed, and for the short time she remained in the grip of this I was stricken with the knowledge that there was nothing on earth I could do to reach her.

It passed. The nurse came. She made my mother an

appointment with her doctor for the following day. For the rest of that afternoon, my mother was lucid, but so cold that she shivered for hours. I brought her blankets and made her cups of hot tea. She was like someone who'd descended frostbitten from high altitude, the chill gone so deep in her it had to work its way out. I sat on the edge of the bed. It looked like there was nothing but a few sticks under the blanket, arranged haphazardly. When I lifted the covers to put heavier socks on her, she raised her head slightly to watch. Some days before, she had banged her calf on the coffee table, and a purple-black bruise had spread violently on the surface of her skin.

'Talk to the doctor about that, too,' I said.

'Mmm . . .' she said vaguely, gazing at the leg with bemusement, as though it were not of her.

The next day she seemed herself again. She said I should stop fussing, I was making her feel like an invalid.

'I'm old,' she said tartly. 'Things happen.'

When I asked her if this particular thing had ever happened before – I'd already noticed she didn't like to use the word *stroke* – she said, 'Not that I know of.' She said it with such false nonchalance I felt sure she was lying.

She sent me out for a few groceries. It was a test. In order to pass I had to show that I was not afraid to leave her alone. She needed to know this. She told me to take the car, but I wanted to walk, much to her bafflement. My mother was not lazy, but she was very American in ways and viewed any walking that was not solely for pleasure as somehow debasing, or even dangerous.

All up and down the street, the buildings were pink and yellow. The sky was a sharp periwinkle blue. There were no clouds, nor was there a breeze. I heard no human voices. Enormous palm trees shaded the big, wide boulevards. The only movement was the slow glide-by of huge sedans and SUVs. A curious, unearthly calm blanketed the neighbourhood. At a random point, the sidewalk ended, and I trudged the grassy verge, feeling conspicuous, as though I were a refugee or a fugitive. When I returned to my mother's, laden with more than I'd intended to buy, she cooed over me as though I had survived some gruelling journey.

I made us lunch and afterwards she sat in her soft chair in the living room with a crossword on her lap, watchful and mostly silent. She seemed different — remote, detached — and I worried that this was not a fleeting mood but the result of damage to her brain. In myself I observed a peculiar unease, a feeling that I'd trespassed on her deepest privacies by witnessing the indignity of her befuddlement, what was surely a milestone in her progress towards death.

The days or weeks between meetings with Cauley were spent in a state of nervous anticipation in which I wished, desperately, to be assured that I was gambling wisely and well. I would fall prey to the fear that our next rendezvous would surely be the moment when the whole thing went flat before our eyes. Then the day would come, the minutes ticking towards his appearance until, finally, there he was. And always there was a sense of – it is hardly too strong a word – *horror*. Not horror at him, exactly, but horror at my own foolishness: that I had allowed the effects of this thing to become so disproportionate to their cause. I suppose they were unavoidable, those moments of deflated rapture.

On one of these occasions, we were to meet in a pub on Chatham Street. Dublin still felt like a foreign country to me, exotic and perilous, and with a language and customs all its own. I couldn't get a clear sense of it, all the leafy squares and the Georgian grandeur, and at the same time something recalcitrant and primal, the side streets still with a tenement-era reek about them. I made my way on foot from Connolly station, crossing the river and stopping at a newsagent's on Grafton Street. As I came out, a skinny young man strode past me, his eyes doing a sweep of the crowd. He had a filthy blanket clutched at his neck like a cape and such an air of purpose about him he looked like a dystopian superhero.

Cauley was in the pub when I arrived. It was almost 6 p.m., late in August. Grotty light streamed in through the stained glass. I saw him before he saw me. He was reading a magazine, one leg crossed over the other, a pint on the table. Whatever way the sun was hitting him, he looked practically translucent. It spooked me. I had my usual moment of doubt, but stronger this time, and different in kind: a sudden, stark dread. A shiver passed through me, a tickle at the top of my spine. I could've been staring at a stranger.

For a split second I thought that I was capable of it after all, of letting him go. In fact, I felt like fleeing. I actually considered it. I saw myself going straight back to the station and getting on the next train west.

Cauley looked up, too quickly, and caught my expression. This was normally the point at which the horror would soften into a feeling of uncertain alarm, and then into shyness. When I would go to him and he would put his arms around me and rub his rough cheek gently against mine, a creaturely gesture I adored, and the doubt would evaporate.

None of that happened, though. He didn't rise to reassure me. Instead I saw alarm in his own eyes and knew that my expression had given me away.

I walked over to him.

'What's wrong?' he said, standing.

I said something about colliding with a junkie.

'Oh,' he said, and seemed to relax a little. 'Are you okay?' He put his hand on my arm and went to kiss me, and I turned aside and said, 'Can you get me a drink?'

By the time he came back with my pint he looked nervous and distant. It seemed that a moment's wavering from me was all it took for his own misgivings to break the surface, for love's false floor to be revealed.

It was a terrible evening, the only truly terrible evening we ever had. At dinner, he worked very hard to make conversation, and I sat there, coldly, observing him.

Finally, he got tetchy. 'What is with you tonight?' he said.

And I said something stupid, like, 'I'm not always a laugh a minute.'

'I don't expect you to be a laugh a minute.'

'Well, then.'

'Well, then, what?'

'Then let me be.'

'But why won't you talk to me about it?'

'About *what*?'

And around and around we went, until our plates were cleared and he paid the bill. I watched and thought, *It's killing him, paying the bill*, and instead of offering to help, which I always did – an awkward gesture, because of course some of my playing-around money was Eddie's – I sat there watching him, pitying him, enjoying his diminishment. A meanness had surfaced in me and I felt helpless to rein it in. He left an excessive tip, to spite me, I thought, and we exited the restaurant in single file, like some old married couple grown sick of the sight of each other.

When we got outside I steered him into the mouth of an

alleyway, pushed him up against the wall and kissed him ardently, a kiss that he returned in kind.

'Let's go to my place,' he said, a fistful of my hair in his hand, his lips thick at my ear.

When we got to the bedsit, it felt all wrong. Everything that had moved me – the humble collection of dress shirts, hung with such care; the accoutrements of creativity and the quiet heroism of artistic struggle they bespoke; the very neatness of the place – now struck me as simply sad. All I could see was cheap cabinetry and curtains that needed cleaning. We tripped towards the bed and had raunchy, untender sex, the kind that would've thrilled us had we not been in the grip of resentment. Afterwards I curled into a ball and cried, feeling sloppy and tragic, while he lay there staring at the ceiling, scratching lazily at his chest.

In the morning, I woke sticky with the heat. The usual sounds were rising from the street. I put on one of Cauley's shirts and sat up in front of the window and peered out at grubby Rathmines. Dublin is miserable in the rain, but unambiguous sunlight doesn't flatter it either. It's a city that is at its best under florid, tumultuous skies, or at sunset on a summer evening, when the light rolls in low from the west and all the filth is hidden in shadow and the river gleams.

Cauley wasn't there. He might've been in the bathroom down the hall, or he might've gone out for the paper – he always woke early. I flopped back down on the bed, a film of sex on my skin, and thought of Eddie. I felt, as insupportable as it sounds, betrayed by him. For knowing what I was doing and not confronting me, for thinking he could just carry on, blow past it or wait it out, for letting me stew here in this awful little trap I had built for myself. A wave of nostalgia rolled over me, a yearning for something wholesome, for him. I thought of a certain autumn afternoon. We were on a weekend break at a restored stately home, and we had rented bikes and ridden on a path that followed a river. It was getting near to dinnertime and we decided to forgo the five-course meal that awaited us, going instead to a pub that served steak and chips. A smell of fried food was leaching from the kitchen. Two men at the next table ate steaks even bigger than ours, holding their knives like pencils and not saying a word to each other but keeping their faces to their plates until I thought they'd lick them clean. I think there was a time in this country when no one spoke, just sat there in a savage silence.

Eddie and I had to cycle home in the dark – he went in front and warned me if there was a tree root or a bend in the path – and when we finally got back to our hotel we ordered whiskeys and nestled by the fire, two people who knew exactly what they meant to each other and revelled in the knowledge.

Cauley came in with the papers and a pint of milk. When he looked at me I saw a trace of affection, and I offered him one of those sheepish smiles that stop just short of apology. I got up and put the kettle on. We didn't say much. We were both hungover, headachey and spent. When we brushed against each other we flinched and said, 'Sorry', as though our actual flesh were tender to the touch. We drank Nescafé and cooked rashers on the portable stove, and I nearly forgot that this was where he lived. The room seemed like a stage set to me, provisional and laid on, as though the dishes, the furniture, the tea towels – all of it, down to the box of tissues on the side table – had been arranged for our use and would be stowed again at the conclusion of our run. I had thought, the first time I visited Cauley, that he'd imposed order on the place on my account. But later I realized it had nothing to do with me. There was something in it that spoke volumes about Cauley, an air of white-knuckled necessity. It was how I imagined a soldier's tent might feel, its order a stay against the outside world, or the inner maelstrom.

I felt a strong need to be out of there.

I said, 'I have an idea. Let's go to Rosses Point.' We were sitting at the table, leafing through the papers and gnawing at some toast, my anxiety building. I wanted to leave. But I didn't want to leave Cauley. I wanted two mutually exclusive things: to flee and to be cocooned, to rid myself of Cauley while pulling him close.

He looked up from the paper. '*What?*'

'We could stay with Kevin.' Kevin who had introduced us, who knew all about us, because Cauley had told him.

He gave me a frigid little smile and said, in a tone he might've employed with a child, 'That sounds like a really bad idea. Why do you want to do that?'

'Eddie is in England,' I said. 'We'll go straight to Kevin's. We won't go into town at all. I want to get out of Dublin.'

He eyed me, steadily. He was right, it was a bad idea; maybe it was even a test — of him, or of us, or of myself. We sat for a while in silence, staring at the tabletop. He was weighing it all up. He was afraid I was leaving him; I could nearly smell the fear off him. And yet I was insisting he come with me, back into the belly of my life. He could either let me go, there and then, and that might be the end of it, or he could say yes and see where I was leading him.

'You know I'm nearly skint,' he said.

'My ticket is for tomorrow. I'll have to buy another anyway. I can buy yours.'

'No,' he said.

After a minute or two I got up and began to gather my things. I wasn't going to leave, just like that, but I needed to occupy myself.

'Let me see what I can do,' he said.

He got up and went to the hall, where the pay phone was, but I didn't hear him speak.

'PJ isn't picking up,' he said, when he came back. PJ was a friend of his, and one of the few things I knew about him was that he had a proper job. I was leaning against the kitchen unit, drinking a cup of water. Cauley took the cup from my hand and set it down and put his arms around me. All the tenderness that had been missing the night before flooded in now. Maybe we saw ourselves coming to an end. Or maybe we thought it was finally getting real. The feel of him was good, and I pressed my hips against his, and he sighed. He let his head fall back and I nipped gently at his exposed neck.

'Okay,' he said, and kissed my forehead, and went out to the pay phone again.

When he came back, he said, 'I'll get some cash, and we'll go.'

And that was how I met his mother.

Cauley's parents, long separated, were the inverse of that old trope of the Irish marriage, the drama of male misconduct and female martyrdom, often hinging on drink. I never met his father, but I gathered he was a steely, inward-looking man. Cauley thought there was a woman he spent time with, but back then, especially down the country, anything resembling life after marriage was viewed as a little shabby or ignoble and wasn't always talked about.

Maeve, Cauley's mother, was some kind of civil servant. She had left Cauley's father some years ago, and though Cauley had never said that she'd left him for Tom, the man she was now living with, I sensed that was the case. Cauley didn't like Tom, and I think he didn't want to admit that this was the man for whom his mother had thrown away the family.

Tom was from Longford, and he owned a breaker's yard out near Swords. I imagined him in a pair of greasy coveralls, enormous oil-blackened hands. Cauley's mother I pictured heavily made up, jagged and slatternly.

We had arranged to meet them at a pub in . . . was it Inchicore? Phibsborough? Terenure? I can't remember. Those places were indistinguishable to me then, blending together in a sea of pebbledash and red brick and illogical traffic flows.

I can recall that pub's interior, though, like it was yesterday. It was just after noontime. The August sun was pouring through the open doors like divine light. A smell of stale beer rose from the dark floorboards; cigarette smoke drifted lacily past. The place was empty but for Maeve and Tom and two older men sitting at a corner table, and all four of them were smoking.

Cauley and I had taken the bus instead of splurging on a taxi. We'd sat on the very front bench, upstairs. I had wanted to sit there for the view – the double-deckers were inordinately thrilling to me – but that day it was all too much. I felt queasy and vertiginous, pitched headlong on to the streets, which vanished in a rolling motion underneath us, as though we were co-pilots losing altitude at a furious rate. Then again, everything felt vertiginous during those days. I had always imagined adultery would feel shadowy and whispered, a world in black and white, all cobblestone and dripping eaves, but what it felt like was being always on the run, everything breathless and fractured and a bit ridiculous.

Maeve and Tom were sitting at the bar. Neither of them bore any resemblance to my imaginings. Tom wore a golf shirt and pressed slacks. There was a slight air of the spiv about him, the snake-oil salesman. He might once have been handsome, in a hale, seafaring sort of way, but his face had acquired the reddish-purple hue of high blood pressure and dissipation. He struck me as a man slightly ashamed, whose manner of surviving that had been to adopt an awkward bravado, unconvincing even to himself. As for Maeve, she looked much like every other middle-aged Maeve I had encountered: a sturdy matron in slacks and blouse and, pinned to her heaving bosom, an amoeba-shaped brooch.

Tom saw us first and called out too loudly, 'There they are!' Maeve turned, blew a jet of smoke towards the yellowed ceiling and looked us over for a moment before saying gently to her son, 'Hiya, pet.'

She gave me a glassy little smile. 'And you're Alice,' she said, as though assigning parts in a school play. She stubbed out her cigarette and didn't offer her hand.

Tom shook my hand, over-eager, compensating for Maeve's coolness.

'Sit,' Tom said, 'sit. What are you having?'

Cauley had told me that we would have to have a drink with them, that he couldn't just borrow money from his mother and leave. So we took the stools beside them, ordered pints, and proceeded to talk about absolutely nothing. I mean, we talked about the traffic that had made us late getting there, and then about some match – I wasn't even sure what sport was at issue – and of course we talked about the weather, though by then the summer's unending sun was a fairly worked-through topic and the collective sense of wonder had been replaced by feelings of fatigue and unreality.

And then Tom said to Cauley, 'How's the scribbling?' and winked at me. Maeve looked hard at her son – I could tell she took his writing seriously.

Cauley tipped his head quickly, dismissively, and turned pointedly away from Tom. 'You know yourself,' he said.

'I don't,' Tom said. He looked at me. 'I loved Shaw as a boy.'

'You're working hard,' Maeve said to Cauley.

Tom said, to no one in particular, 'We who tread the boards are not the only players of parts in this world.'

Cauley still refused to look at him. 'That wasn't Shaw,' he said, sounding bored.

I pitied Tom. I think what he wanted was to package up this mixture of admiration and resentment that he felt for what Cauley did – this thing that mattered to him and that it seemed he had a talent for but which made him so little money he had to come begging to his mother – and to deliver it in the form of a cutting aside. But he wasn't clever enough, or sufficiently clear-headed, to pull it off.

Maeve was harder to read. I wasn't sure what kind of face I should be putting on. Contrite? Deferential? Ashamed? Or, on the contrary, *un*ashamed? I intended to love and honour her son. But could I really do it? I had no idea. I had no idea what I was made of.

She asked me a single question: 'Are you in Dublin for long?'

I fumbled the response. 'Heading home today,' I said, then attempted to correct myself. 'Heading back . . .' The symmetry was making us all a bit queasy. She caught me watching her a few times. The question *I* wanted to ask was: *What's it like, leaving your husband?*

She was reserved, wry, vaguely disapproving. They were both disapproving. But it wasn't our affair they objected to so much as it was our happiness, and probably our youth – that we were young enough to believe that whatever we were feeling really mattered, to think that none of this had ever happened to anyone before, not in the way it was happening to us. They resented the flighty, brazen way we were hurling ourselves at life. They resented our ignorance of each other and ourselves. It wasn't that Maeve and Tom didn't love each other – I think they did. But there was a current of weariness and cynicism running between them. They were deeply, committedly, alcoholic, and in on it together: the grim enterprise of being themselves. It wasn't only the drink, though, that dishonoured them, it was the legal limbo of the undivorced. They had about them a whiff of statelessness, a fugitive air, and an uncertainty about how much their transgressions mattered.

At some point, a signal must've passed between Cauley and his mother because she slipped him a wad of notes, and we all glanced quickly around, as though something crooked were taking place. The whole encounter felt like a burlesque of the classic meeting with a lover's parents, where instead of offering you living proof that love lasts and esteem endures, instead of welcoming you to the land of long-term commitment, they press fifty quid into your hand and tell you to keep your head down.

After an hour or so we made our excuses. Cauley kissed his mother on the cheek, and I shook Tom's hand and half bowed to Maeve, as though she were a cleric – she still seemed disinclined to touch me – and off we flew. I see us running down the street, running as though to catch the last-ever bus, running as though we'd just robbed a bank and our whole mad, vibrant lives were about to begin. We weren't actually running, of course; of that much I'm certain. It was another hot day and neither of us was the least bit fit. But I remember it that way because that was how it felt – like we had so much life in us we couldn't contain it. Of course, we were running from ourselves, too. No great powers of deduction were required to recognize that we had just been presented with a version of our future – it was the sort of thing Cauley might've called, in one of his theatre reviews, a gross over-signification.

As we tumbled into our seats on the bus, he said, with that laconic jocularity that was his dominant register, 'Well, there's us in thirty years!' And we laughed with relief, as though the voicing of it had rendered it impossible. I pressed my head into the crook of his shoulder and ran the tip of my tongue slowly up the side of his neck, which was damp with the heat. He stopped laughing and slid a hand between my legs. I put my arms around him and we held each other, with our eyes closed, waiting for the future to recede.

By the time we drew away from each other, the shadows of his mother and Tom were gone and we were only ourselves again. I kissed him hungrily, and then, though there were two women about ten rows back, I raised myself up and straddled him and we ground slowly into each other. Our encounter with dissipation had only left us feeling lustier and more alive, and for a few moments we could not conceive of it – either of growing old or of seeing our spiritedness, our exuberance, reduced to the sad habit of spending long, bright Saturdays getting wearily blotto.

We got off the bus at the station and from there boarded the train west, the heat waning sweetly and the air turning pure and fresh, confirming our exit from the sordid city. The world was one big, pathetic fallacy to us, and we had never felt so favoured as we did at the outset of that last journey, the sky blue and enormous, the countryside opening like a promised land to receive us.

Kevin's house was a humble little place on a quiet laneway in Lower Rosses, overlooking a beach of pure white powder, one of many unsuspecting properties around there that would soon be worth a fortune. The Point was only on the brink of development that summer. The yacht club had long existed, but there were certainly no yachts there. There were not yet McMansions, there was no spa or leisure centre, no kite-boarding school. It still had the ramshackle feel of an old seaside village.

When we pulled up in the taxi Kevin opened the front door and ushered us in with downcast eyes and an almost reverential air, as though we were on the run from baleful enemies and he was honoured to offer us safe haven. Before he closed the door he stared intently out at the taxi, which was idling on the roadside. I could see he was enjoying the part Cauley had asked him to play.

Kevin worked on building sites. He was a bachelor and a hoarder, and he drank too much. Cauley had told me that when they were in their teens, Kevin had, over the course of one summer, progressed from social to often solitary drinking. A couple of years later a woman he'd hoped to marry left him over it. Kevin had tried and failed twice to get sober. Since then his life had grown small around him. His eyes were glassy and a little elsewhere. The house was in disarray. In the spare bedroom, where we would stay, as well as piles of discarded clothes, several empty stout bottles and some faded paperbacks lying every which way, as though they'd been flung aside in disgust, there were three large triangles of broken glass, from a window or a picture frame, which Kevin had taken care to prop against a wardrobe. He saw me looking at them and said he'd been meaning to remove them.

'I'm cooking chops in an hour,' he said. 'There's plenty.'

I thanked him, and Cauley said, 'Cheers, man.'

He backed out with what was nearly a bow, and Cauley and I sat beside each other on the bed.

'Do you think he minds?' I asked.

'Why should he mind?' Cauley said, and I remembered that men were different.

Across the room, opposite the bed, was a picture window. We could see in the distance the long mountain that loomed behind my own house. It looked like a reprimand. I got up and closed the curtains, which were actually lace, pushed Cauley back on the bed and lay down beside him. We didn't speak. It felt as though we were both waiting for something to happen. We were here. Now what?

Kevin served lamb chops and mashed potatoes, and we ate outside and afterwards sprawled in the front yard, drinking cans of Heineken, our dinner plates scattered like frisbees on the grass. The air had cooled, and we smoked lazily and stared up at the sky. I reached over and ran my finger along the curve of Cauley's jaw. He let his head loll to the side and we gazed at each other until I couldn't take it any more and turned away.

Just after eight, we rose, drowsily, and Cauley suggested

walking to the beach for sunset. Kevin said he'd do the washing-up, but we made him come with us. We were trying to feel it wasn't wrong, what we were doing, that we were just three friends knocking around, and we wanted it to look that way.

We headed down the lane, and then along a path, till we got to the third beach just as the sun was sinking. We could see Lissadell across the inlet to the north and, to the west, the bay opening out into the Atlantic. There were whitecaps in the distance. I put on a pair of red-lensed sunglasses I had found on the floor in our bedroom. They made the few clouds on the horizon – which to the naked eye looked grey and tufty, like what you'd see along the skirting boards of an unswept room – glow like hot coals or swirling lava, what I imagined the end of everything might look like.

When we got back to the house a grainy twilight hung in the sitting room. Cauley got cans from the fridge and the three of us sat talking till late, Cauley and I curled up on the sofa. We had never been in a house together. We had never displayed ourselves so openly, as a couple. We felt drained and content, as though this happiness were an actual accomplishment of ours. We were self-satisfied and insular, radiating benevolence but interested, really, only in ourselves. My marriage, Eddie, the home we shared – those things barely impinged. Honestly, it was as though I thought I could forget my life, collapse it like a piece of furniture and stow it for the season.

In the morning, Cauley and I woke to the chirping of birds. We could feel a light breeze through the open window, and the freshness made the room look all the more sordid. For whatever reason, we had not seen fit to move the triangles of broken glass to a safer spot, and we were lucky that in our nocturnal stumblings to the bathroom we had not gored ourselves. Cauley christened the room the City of Glass, and naming it seemed to domesticate the danger.

We made coffee and stayed in bed till noon. We talked about everything but the situation we were in. We talked about the summers he'd spent in Sligo as a child, and about his mother and my father and all the ways people fuck up their children, even when they're not bad people. We talked about whether we drank too much, and then about the script he was writing – a black comedy about an Irish thug in Marbella who ends up raising a little girl, which sounded to me like a remake of *Paper Moon*. We talked about books, too – or he did, for Cauley was far better read than I – about Philip K. Dick and Borges and other writers I knew nothing about, and we talked about love. He quoted something from the letters of Katherine Mansfield, about how she thought that romantic love was the act of faith that had replaced God, and that what we wanted from the beloved was to be known as we once believed God knew us.

He looked at me to see if I agreed, or if this was what I expected from him.

'You've read the letters of Katherine Mansfield?' I asked.

'More or less,' he said.

When we heard Kevin moving about, we dressed and went to join him. We found him standing in the middle of the kitchen, scratching his head and looking around him like

167

he'd never seen the place before. The tap was turned on full. Cauley shut it off. There was an open can on the table, which I thought was from the night before until Kevin picked it up and took a long swallow from it.

Cauley back-handed him gently in the gut and said, 'I'll make us some breakfast.'

After breakfast we sat around in the shade on the small back patio, reading bits to each other out of a week-old *Irish Times*. Finally, Kevin said he was going to walk over the field to the pub that faced the harbour on the other side of the Point, and we said we would go along. We set out buoyantly enough, but the sun was intense and our initial brisk gait soon degenerated to a trudge. The air wavered in the heat. I was a few steps behind the two of them, the sweat rolling off them and their pale skin so unsuited to the sun I imagined it erupting into blisters right before my eyes. For whatever reason, I thought of Cauley in New York, nineteen years old, the story he'd told me about his one stab at the city. I was thinking how out of character it seemed that he'd given up, but maybe that was what was driving him now, maybe he'd spend the rest of his life making up for it. I was thinking how easily things can go otherwise, how he could be living a life in New York now instead of schlepping across a field with the bay just beyond the rise and me behind him.

Upon arriving at the pub, we collapsed dramatically at a picnic table in the gravel yard. It was a Sunday, and in the fine weather the place was packed. Of course, we saw people we knew. But we seemed to think we were invisible – invisible as lovers, at least, because we had Kevin as a foil, and because no one looked askance at us, and no one asked where Eddie was. I still didn't get it, how much was observed but unspoken, and how little relation whatever did get said bore to what was known or surmised. And so we made merry, digging our own graves and smiling all the while.

It wasn't late, maybe eight o'clock, when we got a lift back to Kevin's. I went into the bedroom and lay down on the tangled sheets. Cauley and Kevin were sitting out front on plastic chairs, and I listened to the hum of their voices and felt consoled. I thought: *I could do this for ever; lie here, listening to him, nothing required of me and nothing wanting.* I felt a complete absence of ambition, I mean even the ambition to go to him. I thought: *He is mine*, and was astonished by my luck.

That was what I was thinking about – my luck – when the phone rang.

It took a moment for me to recognize what I was hearing, it seemed like ages since I'd heard a phone ring, but when I realized what the sound was I was sure it must be Eddie calling. I had phoned our house that afternoon, before we'd gone to the pub, and left him a message, knowing he wouldn't be back till the evening. I'd told him where I was. I'd said that a bunch of us had come here for a party, a bonfire on the beach, and that I would be home tomorrow. I had left him Kevin's number; it would've seemed odd not to.

Now, I scurried to the entryway and stared at the phone. Kevin ambled in from outside and, when he saw me, he hesitated. 'Right,' he said, and went back out the door. The answering machine clicked on and Eddie's voice came through, as crisp and level as a pilot's. He said that he was back and that he could pick me up and that I should let him know when I got in.

When the message ended I went into the kitchen and fished a can of Heineken out of the fetid chaos of Kevin's refrigerator and sat there in the semi-dark, my heart racing from the shock of Eddie's voice. I imagined phoning him, and saying, *Yes, do*, *come for me*, and slipping out the kitchen door and back to him, now, quietly, before it was too late. And in the next moment all I wanted was to hide, to never leave this house or go back to that one. I thought maybe it could be as simple as drawing a line under one life and beginning another.

I heard Cauley and Kevin coming into the sitting room from outside. Cauley called my name, then wandered into the kitchen and said, 'What are you doing in the dark?' He stood behind me and rubbed my shoulders, and a wilting sensation came over me, but when I didn't answer, he stopped. He leaned closer and whispered, 'What's going on?'

'Nothing,' I said. I put my hand over his and didn't look up.

'Nothing?'

'Eddie phoned.'

His grip on my shoulders slackened.

'Just leave me for a bit,' I said.

Kevin came in then, and Cauley straightened and mumbled something to him. Kevin said something back, and opened the fridge and got them each a beer. Then they left the room, quietly and with an almost professional discretion, as though my marriage were a medical condition I was better off attending to in private.

Until the moment I heard his car in the drive it hadn't occurred to me that Eddie would come to Kevin's. I was still sitting in the kitchen, and Kevin and Cauley were in the front room. I got up to go outside – I didn't want Eddie coming into the house – and the two of them watched me cross the room as though they were seeing a ghost. I met Eddie in the drive, and we stood looking at each other. He tipped his head towards the car and said, with no particular inflection, 'Come home. Looks like the party is over.'

When I didn't say anything Eddie walked to the edge of the drive and peered up the lane, just for something to do. It was a gorgeous evening – balmy air, deep-pink skies, a few puffy clouds to the west. I followed him a few steps and sat on the wall that enclosed Kevin's yard. Eddie turned back but didn't sit. He stood there with his hands on his hips.

'Come home,' he said again.

I hesitated, and to my own surprise said, 'What will you do if I don't?'

I don't know what I meant by that, exactly. I wasn't issuing a challenge, and I don't think I meant *ever*. Perhaps I wanted him to say: *Take all the time you need*. Or to assure me that there would be no consequences.

He sighed and looked down at his feet. I could feel Cauley in the house behind us. 'I don't know what I'll do,' he said.

A car rolled past, slowly, and we both stared after it.

'I need to gather my things.'

'Okay,' he said, and turned towards the car.

'I want you to go ahead. I'll be there shortly. I'll call a taxi.'

He turned back to me, irritated. 'That's silly.'

Was it? I didn't know any more what we were pretending and what was simply going unsaid.

'I'll wait,' he said again.

And again I said no. 'I'll be home. I promise.'

His expression changed then, to something like disgust.

Kevin's house was nearly dark inside. Cauley followed me into the bedroom. The sound of the car grew fainter, then disappeared.

Cauley tried to turn on a lamp, but the bulb popped. He cursed and switched on the ceiling light, which must've been about ten watts. 'What happened?'

I lied to him. Or maybe I didn't. Because already I wasn't sure I could do what I'd promised Eddie I would. I slipped my arms around his waist, and he returned the embrace, though tentatively.

'I'm not sure what happened,' I said. 'I don't know what he knows.'

I said that we'd argued about my going home, and then he'd driven off. Cauley waited for me to say more. Poor Cauley. He must've felt the weight of it, Eddie's arrival, and his departure, and the fact that I was still here. He pulled me closer and stroked my hair very gently, and although it seems cheap to claim it, I think we felt, in that moment, ennobled. For all the lies and the guilt and the selfishness, we believed this was a situation we were equal to. That we wouldn't leave each other in the lurch. We stood embracing in the gloom, afraid to speak, awed by what we'd done.

Just after midnight, I called a taxi from Kevin's phone. Cauley was asleep. When I came back into the room I had to turn on the ceiling light to find my things.

Cauley woke and sat up in the bed and squinted at me, confused. 'What are you doing?' he said. 'Are you leaving?'

I was picking my belongings up off the floor – a hairbrush and underwear, a T-shirt, a skirt, two books. How had I scattered so much in such a short time? In the near-dark I nearly walked into the glass propped against the wardrobe.

'Jesus.'

'Be careful,' Cauley said. He got out of bed and went to the window and lifted the curtain daintily. He thought Eddie had come back. Seeing nothing, he turned around and shook his head, still half asleep. 'What the fuck?'

I stopped what I was doing and stood in the middle of the room, in the middle of the mess, and tried to keep from losing it entirely.

'Can we talk tomorrow?' I said finally. 'Can you call me tomorrow?'

He had moved to the bedroom doorway, where he was leaning in the shadows, his arms crossed over his chest, as though he was going to block my path. I wondered if he was capable of that. 'Why did we come here?' he asked.

'Why did we *come* here?'

'Yeah. Why did we come here?'

I looked at the floor. I knew what he was accusing me of – of having delivered us to Eddie. Of creating the conditions whereby Eddie could carry me off, like a trophy. But that was crediting me with more forethought and strategizing than I was capable of. If I can say one thing in my favour with regard to those days, it's that I had no idea, from one hour to the next, what I was doing.

I said nothing. Anything I said would be the wrong thing, and it wasn't like I knew the answer. I zipped my bag shut. In the bedroom doorway I stopped and rubbed my cheek slowly over Cauley's, which was rough with the need of a shave. One of us moaned, softly, and I'm afraid that it was me.

When I was a girl I had a big cut-away doll's house. I used to squat on my haunches in front of it, arranging and rearranging the furniture, thrilling to the sweep of my perspective. Each room in it was like a museum exhibition, the American home c. 1900 — bare floorboards, the furniture spartan but pretty. Mostly, I felt like the benevolent custodian of my domain, but every so often, on a whim, I would reach in with my giant's hand and cast all of it out upon the carpet — beds and dressers and chairs tumbling from the upstairs rooms as though the earth had shook — so that I could start again.

I felt that urge these last months, or something like it, peering into Eddie's house as though from on high, clicking from image to image, from room to room. I wanted to reach in and rearrange it all, so that when Eddie and his wife came through the door and looked around they would be suddenly unsure of themselves. I didn't want to haunt them, exactly, or to take my husband back. It was more a desire for a rent in the fabric of reality.

I thought I saw him today. Eddie, I mean. He was coming out of Buswells Hotel and he had a little girl with him, she must've been six or seven. He was putting a cap on her head while she stared vacantly across the street with an attitude of forbearance.

My heart began to thrum. My palms prickled. My first instinct was to call his name. Immediately after, I thought to turn away. Instead, I stood there, captivated. He was like a memory given dimensions, a dream made material. I wanted to stare and stare, to stay rooted in the stark sensation of seeing him. And then something in his stance, a turn of his head, and I saw it wasn't him. He took the girl by the shoulders, then buttoned the top button of her coat and straightened the hat and gave her a little rub on the head. He looked left, then right, and they headed off towards Dawson Street.

It hardly surprised me, my mistake. Lately, I've been seeing him everywhere – not thinking it was actually Eddie, as I did this morning, but catching glimpses of him in the profiles and gaits and gestures of other men. I pass a man with a child, and I think about the children Eddie and I didn't have, the ghosts of our unchosen future. I think of the history we didn't accrue, as though it were a country we have yet to visit. I have imagined, in the most absurd and proprietorial way, Eddie in our home, alone, holding down the fort till my return.

We camped once, Eddie and I, on a patch of lakeshore near the Leitrim border. When I woke in the morning a yellowy-green light hung low over the grass and the sky was a powder blue. The lake was blue, too, smooth as a pane, and along the shore reeds pierced the water's surface. I had never seen such stillness. Eddie hadn't woken yet, and I lay there looking at the sky, the sunlight spangling the trees, and felt sorry for anyone who wasn't me.

I think about that day and others like it, when I felt at the heart of the world and wished for nothing more than my life, exactly as it was. I think about why, having found that feeling, I couldn't hold it.

There was a week, between the day I left Eddie and the day I went to Dublin, when I stayed with Jane in Sligo. One afternoon I bumped into Eddie on Quay Street. If you have ever been married and then separated, I hardly have to tell you how disorienting the first chance encounter is. The shock of meeting each other and not saying the most habitual things – about what to pick up for dinner or where the car was parked – was such that I felt utterly severed from him. The marriage, our love, the day-in, day-out intimacy of those years, felt like a dream we'd had together and remembered only hazily, if at all.

I get back to Monkstown around seven o'clock. It is the first evening of the year when there is a perceptible trace of spring in the air. My time in this house is winding down. I have begun looking for somewhere to rent, probably in town. I will stay for a while, I have decided. I will keep working as a consultant. Last week I got an email from an old friend I knew in Kosovo who'd been asked to go back to Priština for six months, to fill a gap. He'd declined and was writing to see if I'd be interested. When I told Harry about the offer, which I didn't intend to accept, he winced. Harry found Kosovo insistently depressing. He said the entire place, even the open fields, even the sunny days, felt dark and cursed. He said the only good thing about Priština was that it was the one city in the world where you could say: *I'll meet you on the corner of Bill Clinton and Mother Teresa.*

I make dinner and read until ten in the sitting room, then

step out back to smoke a cigarette. Overhead, a crosshatch of bare branches against the moonlit sky makes me think of the brain, its axons and dendrites. I hear movement in the darkness, a scuttling in the hedge to the left of me. And then a cat emerges from the shadows. It pauses in the middle of the back garden, its front paw raised, and looks right at me, before vanishing into the opposite hedge. I think of Olivia. She was my cat, but there was no question of my bringing her to Dublin with me when I left. She was a country cat, invigorated by the outdoors. I was in awe of her double life, hunting and killing in the blackest of nights and the next day curled snugly on the sofa, looking pampered as a pasha. Before having her spayed, we had allowed her, one time, to go into heat and to have a litter. I had never seen a cat give birth before and I promised Eddie I'd find homes for the kittens, which, with much effort and cajoling, I did. I don't know what I'd been expecting from Olivia. I suppose I thought going into heat would be a discreet or hidden process, like a woman's menstruation. I wondered if I would even know it was happening. In fact, I was shocked by both the suddenness and the intensity of it. Late one night, she got up from where she lay on the sitting-room rug and headed with her usual mincing prowl towards the front door – she was all business, like when she detected a mouse or a bird in the vicinity, and I assumed that she had murder on her mind. But when she reached the door she stopped, her back arched and her body elongated, tensile. Her rump rose slightly, and the most astonishing sound issued from her: a scalded, involuntary yowl. I had never witnessed anything like it, and what I felt for her was pity. She looked at the door and then back at me, with such imperiousness that in my haste to do her bidding I stumbled. The night was dark purple, and it swallowed her.

Before bed, I brush and floss, attending with unusual care to the ritual. This morning I was at the dentist and am feeling that renewed commitment to my teeth that a good dentist will inspire. My dentist is youngish, mid-thirties. He has a diploma on his wall from Chapel Hill, and we talked about the American South and he told me he loved Faulkner. It was my first time seeing him. I liked him. He wasn't, you know, dentisty. He donned his latex gloves and flexed his fingers like he was about to crack a safe. Then he hooked his thumb under my jaw like a clamp and placed his index finger in my mouth and pressed down on . . . something. A molar maybe, or just the back bumper of a gum. I was wearing those safety glasses, the ones that are always a little greasy. His finger was thick in my mouth, traversing the terrain, probing. I could feel the jelly of my tongue on it. I closed my eyes and tried not to mind about the pleasure. It seems like such a long time since anyone has touched me.

I slept in the spare room the night I came home from Kevin's house. It was on the ground floor, below our bedroom. I left my bag on the table in the hall so that Eddie would know I was home, and I closed the door. When I heard him the next morning, getting ready for work, I didn't venture out and was relieved that he didn't knock.

That day, I tidied up the house. Then I went out front and pulled some weeds from the rockery, while Olivia lay curled under a shrub, sheltering from the sun. After a while, I gave up doing anything and sat in the living room and tried to imagine what would happen when Eddie came home. I thought that within a marriage – I mean, one's own marriage – there are currents that operate independently of us and of which we seem remarkably ignorant. I didn't know what to expect, from either of us. I wasn't sure I knew what I wanted.

I thought of phoning my mother. During the last conversation I'd had with her, she had sensed, not for the first time in recent weeks, that something was wrong. She believed that it had to do with sex. She told me I needed to take care, that I shouldn't give Eddie cause to stray by becoming disinterested, and I had wondered, after hanging up, whether this thing with Cauley was just a cheap solution to a commonplace problem: the anticlimax of settled domesticity. It was a question I had asked myself in the beginning of our affair but that I felt I'd answered, and I was bothered by how the conversation had set me doubting again.

We rarely talked about sex, my mother and I. From the age at which I'd first understood that I had been the product of a brief liaison, I'd had a discomfort with her sexuality that went, I think, beyond the unease people commonly feel about their parents' erotic lives. Because I had no evidence of my parents' prehistory – no photos, for example, of the two of them together prior to my arrival – the one act I could be absolutely sure they had shared in assumed unwelcome prominence in my mind.

I was thinking about all this that afternoon – about my mother and my father and what the two of them had or hadn't meant to each other. I felt a sudden wave of empathy for my mother, for whatever hopes she'd brought with her into my father's bed, and I decided that I would call her. I wasn't going to tell her what was happening. I knew I couldn't bring myself to do that. I only wanted to hear her voice.

I went upstairs to our bedroom, which I had entered only briefly, and uneasily, earlier that day. There was a phone on the bedside table, but instead of dialling I sat down on the bed, which Eddie had made, very neatly. It looked sealed, the way other people's beds do. The sense of trespass was so strong that I felt incited to go further. I wanted to riffle through Eddie's things. I felt the sort of intimacy with him I imagined a thief might feel with the stranger whose bedroom he was burgling. Very slowly, I lay back on the bed, as though unsure it would support my weight. It was about four in the afternoon, the sun was still warm through the big Velux window. There was a glass of water on the bedside table. Eddie's wedding ring was sitting on the window ledge.

I didn't call my mother. I closed my eyes and lay there, the air from outside so clean and light on my skin it was hard to believe there was anything amiss with the world. When finally I stood, I was unsteady, as though the house had tipped on its foundations.

I was in the living room when Eddie came home. He set his briefcase on the floor, dropped into one of the armchairs, folded his hands in his lap and looked at me.

I asked if he wanted a drink, and he said a gin and tonic would be lovely.

In the kitchen, I tried to gather myself. I mixed the drink and took a swallow, then brought it in, placed it carefully in front of him like some housewife from the fifties and retreated to my chair.

'You're not having anything?' he asked.

I shook my head. I already regretted not making myself one, but I was trying to appear virtuous.

He sipped at the drink and winced with pleasure, then set the glass back on the table. He looked ridiculously cool-headed, like someone in a film. 'You were seen, you know.'

It seemed an odd thing to say, and the delivery so out of character, but maybe any opening would've been strange.

'Yesterday?' The word sounded wrong. Was it only yesterday that I had been with Cauley?

'Not yesterday, no.'

'When?' I heard a meekness in my voice that perturbed me. I thought I shouldn't compound my misdeeds by grovelling. I could be nervous, I could even shake, but I shouldn't cringe and I shouldn't cry.

With a flick of his hand he dismissed the question, as though it were a subject we'd already covered.

'Where?' I asked.

He picked up his drink and said nothing.

'You're not going to tell me?'

'Does it matter?'

Did it? I suppose it didn't. What mattered was that he wasn't going to tell me. I wondered was he bluffing. 'Why didn't you say something?'

He let out a long, elaborate sigh, and his whole being seemed to soften with the exhalation. He looked over to where the sliding glass doors were open. 'I was waiting for you to say something,' he said, more gently now, and I almost believed him and was flooded with remorse. It was very effective, whatever he was doing.

Neither of us spoke. We were both staring out the door now, at the rockery and the fence we'd been meaning to replace and the firs that marked the border of our property. I wasn't sure why I'd come back last night, whether out of guilt or fear, or maybe out of love, or the end of love, which is perhaps more powerful, in its way.

'I'm so sorry,' I said.

Eddie gave that little upward tip of his head, the look of martyred acquiescence that covered just about everything. I had no idea whether he meant we should put all this behind us or that we were past the point where apologies could make a difference.

I waited for him to speak.

When he did, he said, 'We should eat.'

'I'm not hungry.'

'You have to eat.' He said it as though I'd been refusing food for days.

'I don't want to,' I said. 'You eat if you're hungry.'

We sat there, in a very focused silence, like two people stumped on a quiz show as the clock ticks. I felt there was something I should say, something specific, that this was the moment when I asked him whether he wanted me to leave, but that seemed more than we were ready for. Eventually, he said that I could do as I pleased but that he needed some dinner, and he got up and went into the kitchen. I retreated to the spare room, where I remained, silent and immobile, as though, if I were quiet enough, he might forget that I existed.

About an hour later I heard him make a phone call, and when he hung up he went out, without saying goodbye. I emerged from the spare room and walked into the hall, and then the sitting room, and then the kitchen. Everything looked different, in a way I couldn't put my finger on, like when you've let people stay in your house while you're away.

Cauley phoned the next morning around eleven. He sounded distant, but intimate, like we were two people touching base after a heist. He didn't ask how I was. He said, 'Did you tell him?'

'I didn't tell him,' I said. 'But he says he's known for a while.'

'How, if you didn't tell him?'

'I don't know,' I said. 'All he'll say is that we were seen.'

'The other day?'

'No. Sometime before. He won't tell me where, or when or who told him.'

Cauley scoffed. 'That's a bit perverse.'

Was it? To me it seemed mean but fair. But that was because I was still assuming that Eddie would tell me sooner or later, and we would go over all the gory details.

'It's not perverse,' I said.

'It's fucked up,' Cauley said, sharper now, and I had the feeling his anger was not on my behalf but was something between himself and Eddie.

I didn't dare ask the obvious: What will become of *us*? It was clear Cauley wasn't going to raise the subject, and I tried not to read too much into that. Maybe he felt I'd made a fool of him the other night and he needed to get back at me. Or maybe he felt me readying to leave Eddie and it frightened him. I didn't know whether to reassure him with proclamations of love or, on the contrary, to play down the intensity of what I was feeling, to promise him I wasn't about to do anything rash, and so I bumbled along in the middle and said nothing that made any sense at all.

He promised to call again as soon as he could, and we hung up.

I read once that to commit to love is to commit to love's diminishment. Which means that commitment is less about optimism than it is about realism — accepting that love is doomed to become less of itself, and proceeding anyway, in the faith that one will be equal to that truth when it arrives.

Eddie and I took a week in Lanzarote once. We were only a few months married, just emerging from the wedding and its afterglow, and entering a new phase, tranquil but eager, in which we lived in the anticipation of our shared future.

We stayed in a big white hotel facing the sea in Puerto del Carmen. In the mornings, the multi-tiered and clattering breakfast room smelled steamy and not altogether fresh, a mix of meat and acrid coffee and bodies not long from sleep — the hirsute men of Mitteleuropa in their netted nylon tops, and their women, bulky and guttural. We spent the first couple of days at the beach, where rows of orange and blue umbrellas ran in perfectly straight lines. Underneath the umbrellas, the women rose darkly like mountain ranges, their tanned breasts slab-like, or globular, or melting back into their bodies. I don't like going topless, even in bed. My breasts feel like cupboard doors left open, things vaguely in the way. But I was in awe of the breasts of these women — these fifty-something women, some even older, born as Europe was rebuilding itself from ruin. I thought that if I were husband to breasts like that, I would be rendered speechless. I pictured those men — not skinny themselves but of far less dramatic proportions than the women – carrying their great big wives through life, hauling them through the years like some kind of plunder they weren't sure what to do with, and I felt envy for them all, for the husbands and wives and their lack of shame, and all that flesh and history.

On the third day, we hired a car to see the island. The roads were smooth and new and there were not many people on them. We drove to the port at Órzola and boarded a day boat to the smaller island of La Graciosa. We passed dull green cliffs that dropped like curtains into the sea. On La Graciosa we bought picnic supplies and rented bikes and cycled the sand-dirt track. As we crested a hill the sea appeared below us, ice-blue and alarming in its beauty. The sun was searingly hot. The powdery sand burned our feet as we galumphed towards the water in our flip-flops. There were a couple of dozen people there, but no one was swimming. At the shoreline, the beach sloped steeply. There were no shallows, just large waves breaking right where the beach began. We waded in to our knees and I felt a fierce pull, and Eddie grabbed my arm and said, 'Don't go further.' We splashed water on ourselves, then got out and found a shaded bench near the path, where we sat like children, side by side, eating our sandwiches and watching the waves. I felt a peculiar sort of loneliness, intense and perilous and somehow related to Eddie, as though my very survival depended on his existence, but I had no way to communicate this, to make him understand it.

Late that afternoon, driving from Órzola back to Puerto del Carmen, we passed through the Volcano Park. The day was cooling, the sun where we could no longer see it. Eddie pulled over on a high lay-by off the twisty mountain road and we got out of the car. Spread before us in the distance was an expanse of black gravel, where succulents flowered violently. It looked like an exposed seabed, fabulous and other-worldly. Eddie got the binoculars from the car and handed them to me before looking himself. When he took his turn to scan the landscape I watched him and was overcome with wonder. What I wanted more than anything just then was to live well with Eddie, by which I meant not only to love each other fully but to become, because we were together, better people. I believed absolutely in the possibility and felt an impatience to begin.

It took about a week for me to understand that Cauley had ended it. He didn't phone the following day, or the day after, or the day after that, and no letter arrived. I tried calling the pay phone in the corridor outside his flat. Once, one of his neighbours answered and said she'd slip a note under his door, but he never rang back. I became convinced that Cauley would ring only if I left the house. And so I would go outside, pull the phone to the very end of its lead and set it on the front step. Then I would attempt to do something — trim the hedge or read or sweep the path, all the while listening for the phone's trill, listening with a kind of suppressed hysteria that embarrasses me still.

I thought of going on the train to Dublin. I tried to tell myself that I had the right, that Cauley's silence left me no choice. I went over and over the things he'd said to me in our last conversation, as though I might divine from them some direction. And then I went over his silence, trying to read it for signs.

In the end, I didn't go to Dublin. I think what stopped me was less the fear that Eddie might lock the door behind me than that Cauley might not receive me in quite the manner I desired.

I'm trying to be honest here.

Finally, I drove to Kevin's house. He invited me in but didn't offer me anything. I glanced around, trying to take in everything, as though I might see some clue to Cauley's whereabouts or thoughts. The house was dark inside; it had lost its love-nest aura and was simply depressing. Kevin, who only a week ago had seemed a benevolent extra in our love story, was now unshaven and shakier than ever.

I asked him if he'd heard from Cauley, and he said he hadn't, but I didn't believe him. I'd had the sense, when Cauley and I were here, that Kevin was relishing his part in our drama, and now, in the aftermath, if that was what this was, he was relishing his new part, which was – what? To witness my suffering? To help keep me in the dark? The boys were closing ranks, and Kevin, I suspect, was not without sympathy for Eddie.

'I just want to know he's okay,' I said, as if it was all about Cauley's well-being and nothing about my needs.

'I'll give him a ring,' Kevin said. 'If I reach him, I'll tell him you called round.'

I tried to linger, in the desperate hope that Cauley might phone Kevin while I was there. But there was nothing else to say and no reason for my hanging on there, and so I mumbled my goodbyes and got back into the car.

It astonishes me now, that I survived those days of unknowing. But people did, back then: there were times when you just didn't know where your loved ones were, when you couldn't reach them and it didn't mean they were dead or had abandoned you.

In the meantime, Eddie and I had conversations. We avoided mentioning Cauley by name, but I felt exposed, utterly without privacy, at the thought that Eddie had been, in some sense, an audience to the affair. Whether out of weakness or faith or apathy, he had allowed it to go on. Oh, I don't mean *allowed*, as though he might otherwise have put me under lock and key; but he'd never said a word. It was impressive, the discipline that must have required. I hadn't gotten involved with Cauley in order to test Eddie — it was enough trying to manage my own impulses and confusion without taking on the inner lives of others. But now that everything had screeched to a halt, I found Eddie's reaction alarming. What I had expected — that he would break down and tell me what he knew, that he would say to me, repeatedly, *how could you?* — wasn't happening. He behaved instead as though it were all simply beneath him, Cauley and I little more than naughty children who had embarrassed him in front of the other grown-ups.

'Were you not going to even mention it?' I asked one evening.

'What did you want me to say? *What are you doing?* I knew what you were doing.'

'Didn't you want to know . . . what was going to happen?'

'Did *you* know what was going to happen?'

I sighed and looked away from him. That's not the point, I thought.

Another time I said, 'Didn't you want to know *why*?'

We were standing in the kitchen. He didn't answer right away. He crossed his arms over his chest and stared blankly at a flayed, half-eaten chicken going coldly greasy atop the stove. The poor thing looked like we'd taken a hammer to it. This discussion had caught us unawares, triggered by a stray comment, and we hadn't steeled ourselves sufficiently. He was raw, and I was speaking rashly.

Finally, he said, 'In a way, I guess I didn't.'

I felt during those weeks that I knew nothing about my husband, because I did not know the most essential thing – whether his steadfast refusal to corner and accuse me had been proof of his love, of his faith and his patience, or whether it meant that he was essentially indifferent to what I did, and that what mattered in the end was only that order should prevail. I believed what Eddie wanted was to forget that any of it had ever happened, when what I needed was an investigation, a verdict, a chance for expiation.

As the days and weeks passed and summer turned to autumn, we grew wearier and more estranged. Eddie's silence seemed to harden, and every day I tried to imagine my future and went blank with panic. One night – it was the last time we went out together socially – we attended a party in the flat-roofed hotel on the bridge. An old friend of Eddie's had returned from America to celebrate the fiftieth wedding anniversary of his parents, a couple who had treated Eddie, when he was growing up, like another son. Eddie insisted I didn't have to come, and I insisted that I wanted to. I think I was trying to stage civility between us, to put us in a situation where we had to act the part. I thought it would give us some relief from ourselves. And though the choice of occasion was a bit masochistic, a fact we acknowledged with the exchange of a brittle little smile, I was trying to feel, too, that I didn't have to hide; lately, I had avoided town as much as possible. There are no secrets in a small Irish town, not for long, and I knew there'd been gossip about us. The previous week, I had met Eddie in town for a lift home, and as we walked from Wine Street to the car park on the quays, I realized that I was trudging behind him, in the manner of a bad dog, and I gave myself a quick mental slap – look sharp! – and straightened up and met the eyes of anyone we passed.

What I remember of the party that evening is a low, red sun, visible from only one corner of the room, through the picture window, but suffusing the whole room, briefly, with a rose-coloured light. I remember feeling cut off from everyone, as though I were behind glass. And I remember a moment when Eddie caught my eye. He was talking to someone, and he offered me the tiniest, most intimate smile, and it was clear that for a split second he'd forgotten the state we were in – it was the old habitual smile, the old warmth – and then, very quickly, the smile vanished and his eyes went blank, and it was as though he were looking right through me.

We didn't stay long, I think we both felt the awfulness of being there. On the way home I said that I was sorry I had gone, and he said that he hadn't forced me, and I said, 'No, I mean I'm sorry – I should have let you go alone. You might've enjoyed it more.'

'I don't think so,' he said quickly. And then, after a moment, 'But you're right, you should have.'

In the end, we simply wore each other out. We agreed that it was over and began the odious task of dismantling our marriage.

The autumn saw us ambushed by nostalgia. I suspect it's not unusual. We were spent and, in our exhaustion, all the minor grievances fell away and a kind of tenderness rolled in. The weather colluded. The heat, which by late August had had us itchy as caged beasts, finally receded. The tar on the roads hardened, the air thinned and grew cool, the earth itself seemed to mellow. In the evenings, the mountain tended towards a pale pinkish-yellow. I had a brief fit of domesticity, as though something in me knew that this would be the last proper home I would have for a long time. I made jam from our own raspberries. I weeded the small front garden. I even sanded down a desk in the shed, something we'd bought one day at an antique shop in Wicklow with the intention of restoring. It was like bad triage – letting the very worst thing happen, while I busied myself with trivialities.

We didn't cook much. Eddie worked late, out of what felt like courtesy, then we'd meet for a bite down in the nearby village, because the thought of facing each other for an entire evening at home cowed us. We were frightened and sad, and we no longer felt easy in our own home. After so long at odds with each other, it felt, bizarrely, that we were in this thing together – the shepherding through of our dissolution – and I had to work not to slide back into love with him.

When I left him that October, I went to Dublin. My mother assumed I'd move back to America after the split, but I felt no desire to do that. It had been seven years since I'd lived in that country, and already I'd lost the sense of it. I think I believed, too, that I didn't deserve such a clean getaway. Ireland felt sticky to me, like a room in a nightmare, a purgatory I had to earn my way out of.

For several bleak months I lived with an austerity that strikes me now as melodramatic, but which I know meant simply that I had no idea how to proceed. I rented a bedsit off Haddington Road. I sent my patchy CV to dozens of media outlets and even some advertising firms. Eventually, I got an admin job for an architectural trade magazine housed in a laneway off Fenian Street. Within a few weeks I was writing product features on wallpaper and timber and floor tiling. I felt moored by the work's banality and the ritual of nine to five. Occasionally, I joined my office mates for after-work drinks, but I always slipped away after the first or second round. I was determined not to lose control. I was trying to put some distance between myself and what had happened.

All around me, I saw the city being gutted and rebuilt. There were cranes that looked like giant scissors, poised to slice the air, and others that stood straight and proud like T-squares, and others that dangled drunkenly. Buildings seemed to vanish overnight, and in their sudden absence I could not remember what had stood in the now-empty spaces. I thought of a day when Eddie and I were heading out of the city, driving towards the N4, towards the setting sun – I had actually been with Cauley that day, I was not long from his bed – and it seemed the streetscape was rising and falling around us as we went. From everywhere at once came the sound of pneumatic drills ripping through concrete, like the rumblings of war. I think we both felt it, the strangeness and the violence of it all, and neither of us said a word.

The winter wore on. At the weekends, people left the city in droves for wherever they came from down the country, and Dublin felt desolate and empty. I'd buy a phone card and call my mother, working hard to sound upbeat, like I was on the cusp of a new life and knew exactly what I was doing. Every time we spoke she said that if it was really over with Eddie, then why didn't I come home, and every time the question was harder to answer. I couldn't say to her – it would've embarrassed me – that I had some notion that there was a nobility in hanging on here, that going back to America would only compound my shame. I thought about Eddie all the time. I wondered how he spent his evenings, what he ate, how he felt when he went to bed at night. I thought of how we never have to face our own absences – the pain they cause, or whatever rushes in to fill the space. I tried not to think about Cauley, then I tried to think very hard about him, as though I could blow a hole right through him and he would disperse, like pollen, and drift away.

It's a cool, low-skied April day. Sooty grey clouds have gathered in a rush and now rain is threatening. Harry and I have just had a sandwich at a coffee shop on Baggot Street and are walking in Merrion Square. We stick to the tree-lined outer path, which even on the sunniest days has an air of brooding and damp. Harry has been talking about his marriage and its demise. The last time the subject came up, he said something about the travelling having taken its toll. He and his wife had met in Tanzania, and she had followed him to his next duty station. But once their daughter was born, his wife had wanted to make a home in Dublin. He stayed on in Tanzania. When I asked him why he hadn't moved back with his wife, he said, 'It was the eighties. There weren't a lot of jobs in Dublin for someone like me. There weren't a lot of jobs full stop.'

Today he says, 'I thought it would be for a year or two, and then I'd come back.' But he delayed. His visits home became fraught. 'I felt in the way. I was convinced she'd fallen in love with someone else.'

'Had she?'

'I think she did, for a time. But the damage was already done.'

I wonder if Harry wanted out, if he chose to absent himself until the marriage was no longer tenable. I want to ask him this. I want to ask why, if the marriage had died, he'd dragged it out like that.

Finally, I say, 'Was there someone else for you, too?'

Harry looks surprised. Till today, we've talked around these things, and what I notice now in my hesitation is less a respect for his privacies than a reluctance to hear him speak longingly of someone else.

'My wife didn't want her life to be following me around while I lived my life. I didn't want that either, but neither of us had figured out how to live otherwise. And by the time we might've learned that, we had both done things that damaged the marriage and pushed us apart.'

I think of my mother, her broken engagement when she was young, the knowing what's not wanted without the knowledge of what is.

I tell Harry about the end of my own marriage, the affair with Cauley, how Eddie couldn't bring himself to talk about it, how I got angrier and angrier.

'So how did it end?' Harry says.

'He asked me what I wanted to do and I said I thought I should go, and he sort of . . . acquiesced.'

'Was it what he wanted, for you to go?'

I think for a moment. It was all so long ago, and I'm not sure I've ever known what Eddie wanted. 'Yes and no, I think.'

'But you did. You wanted to go?'

'I must've,' I say.

Harry offers me a little smile.

'I ended up feeling like he'd watched it go on,' I say. 'The affair, I mean. I hated that. I know this sounds crazy, but I felt abandoned.'

'Affairs have a rather terrifying momentum,' Harry says wryly. 'Sometimes it's wisest to just get out of the way.'

Harry is warming to Eddie, and I can hardly blame him.

'Maybe,' I say. I think of a moment from that summer, one I recall vividly, though nothing else of the evening has stayed with me. Eddie and I were drunk, and I remember his eyes on me, his look of alarm and confoundment, and my own inner state: I felt feral, like an addict, all stealth and unreason. He couldn't have reached me if he tried.

'What happened to the other guy?' Harry asks. 'Did you see him after that?'

'I saw him once,' I say.

It was that winter, a few months after it ended. I had expected to run into Cauley – the city is so small – but as is the way with such things, it didn't happen at any of the moments when I was braced for it. It was on Kildare Street, about four in the afternoon on an unforgiving February day, leaden and grim, a clammy wind blowing. He was coming out of the National Library and I was walking towards Nassau Street. He stopped when he saw me, shifted a canvas bag to the other shoulder and greeted me with excessive surprise. I tried to bandy it back. We both glanced around then, furtive as spies, as though anyone cared any more what we got up to. The last time I'd seen him he was standing in the bedroom doorway at Kevin's house. I had kissed him goodbye, weak with the want of him, and certain that, in that instant, he hated me. Not for going back to my husband, exactly – we hadn't made any promises to each other, nor had we ended anything – but for having pretended that this moment would never arrive, that we could go on playing house for as long as our hearts desired.

And now, here he was, standing in front of me as though none of that had ever happened – as though we hadn't lain in his bed under the open window, slick with our mingled sweat, as though a mere look from the other hadn't rendered us weak-kneed – saying something about Synge, about research he was doing at the library for an adaptation he was hoping to direct.

When he asked what I was doing I said that I was living here now, and he nodded and said he'd heard, but he didn't elaborate. I told him I'd come to Dublin for a job, as though it were some kind of career move. I didn't say that I was answering phones and writing about floor tiles. He nodded vaguely and looked me in the eye. That was the point at which, if one of us was going to say it – that we should talk sometime – it would've been said. But neither of us suggested it. Instead we had a tricky little exchange in which we each managed to determine the direction the other was heading and then said, 'Oh, I'm going the other way' or some such thing, and then we said goodbye, and that was the end of that. We didn't touch, not a squeeze of the hand or a kiss on the check or a consolatory embrace.

I was shaking when I walked away, my whole body, as though I had just witnessed a terrible accident. And yet there was a distinct sense of anticlimax, too. Why is it that what we so often find on meeting someone we've loved seems not a residue or an after-image but a feeling more like foolishness?

I'd stood there, close enough to touch him, and it seemed the moment should have been marked by the opening of the heavens, a clap of thunder – anything but this small, vague embarrassment.

Harry has stopped walking and is staring at one of the benches along the path. There is a woman asleep on the bench, and sitting up beside her, or sort of sitting up, is a man. He is leaning forward, and I think at first that he is actually falling, that he's going to tip head first on to the tarmac path and split his skull. But then I see how slowly he is moving, and I realize he's leaning over, he has his hand extended towards something – a rag, it looks like – lying atop a small canvas satchel on the ground. Down and down he goes, his advance barely perceptible. Midway to his goal, he lifts his head slightly and swivels it tentatively, dumbstruck, as though only having landed on this earth. I wonder if, in the state he's in, the world seems positively frenetic to him as it goes about its business, or if, instead, everything happens at the speed of treacle. Harry and I are engrossed in his progress, but before the man reaches the item he actually falls asleep, gently and seamlessly and rather impressively. He just *freezes*. I feel like clapping, as though we've been watching a piece of improv theatre, and am immediately horrified by the impulse.

Harry and I look away, in opposite directions, shamed, I guess, or sad. Harry told me once about Dublin in the early eighties, when heroin really came on the scene. He had friends in Dún Laoghaire, not far from where I'm staying now, who'd overdosed or died of AIDS. Sometimes Harry's stories about Ireland in the decades before I came here awaken in me a vicarious nostalgia that I can understand only as an aspect of my affection for him.

He tips his head slightly – *shall we?* – and we continue along the path.

A mist is settling in around us. The edges of things are growing furred. The square is nearly deserted. Harry is all in black beside me, from his brogues to his fedora. He looks, in the mist, like a Cold War movie spy. He looks handsome. The last time we had dinner, what I wanted more than anything was for Harry to invite me up to his sixth-floor apartment for a nightcap and let me lie down on his voluminous couch – he's told me he has a black leather couch – while some milky jazz poured from a four-inch-high speaker and a sheen of moonlight spread across the floorboards.

I didn't suggest it.

He says, 'When my father died, I felt a great need to put my life in order, to clarify things. I felt my mortality.'

'Is that what I'm doing?' I say. 'Feeling my mortality?'

'Nothing wrong with that,' he says, smiling. 'We've got to feel it sometime.'

'True,' I say. But I don't know if I am doing that. I know that a certain pressure has leached from my grief. Its demands are easing. My mother's death is no longer an instant or a day and the shock that reverberated out from that. It is who I am now, the bearer of her story, her life and the end of it. It has been seven months and as many days since she died. Sometimes I forget, by which I mean not only that the thought comes to me that I must give her a call, but that I forget my own sadness, as though it is an item I have left the house without. I find myself in the midst of a moment of unaccountable delight, and then I remember that my mother is dead, and I think: *Why am I not felled by this? Why are we not all, all the time, crippled by grief?*

'So did you clarify things?' I ask.

Harry stops, turns to me. 'Some things,' he says. 'Others I just let go.'

The mist is growing denser, saturating. We shelter under a tree, which doesn't much help.

'Look,' Harry says, 'the laburnum are coming into flower.' And he gazes out over the square with satisfaction, as though he had ordered the spring himself and here it was, arriving.

Towards the end of my mother's life, and especially after Stan died, I used to feel, each time I left her, as though I'd failed her in some way. I looked at her with a kind of broken-heartedness, because it was never enough, what I did. I could not save her from this life, or from death. I would go on living in her absence, and this, we all know, is a betrayal. But death is a betrayal, too. One has done it, one has crossed over, as though to the enemy's side. We were all in this together, and then suddenly we weren't.

The day she died, I was in a taxi coming back from Jomo Kenyatta. My mobile rang and it was a woman who lived in my mother's building, her closest friend there, whose number my mother had recently insisted on giving me. We spoke briefly, about when and how it had happened, and I said that I would call her when I got back to my house.

I rang off, and when I looked up I caught the taxi driver's eye in the rear-view mirror. I held his gaze. My mouth was hanging open a little. For a moment, I felt terribly close to him. I felt he understood everything, and that I did, too, and that the two of us were keepers of a truth so shattering we didn't dare speak it. When I turned to the window the world looked distant and inscrutable to me, as though I'd been decoupled from it.

I spent five days in my mother's condo after her funeral. I was overcome with inertia and didn't want to leave. I sat on the sofa at night, where my mother and Stan had sat so many nights, where I had sat with them, the three of us in a row, the HD glaring out at us, and I wanted to sink into the every-thing and the nothing that was left. I kept the television off and ate my dinner in silence, and felt such a sense of after-math I half expected to lift my head and see the living room strewn with wreckage. Instead I saw a line of paired shoes through the bedroom door. I saw the framed photos fanned atop the wooden console and my mother's ancient desktop Dell. I saw the gewgaws on the side table, a collection of finger-high elephants. My mother used to say, in her later years, 'Don't buy me anything, I'm trying to shed stuff.' And she had, and so coolly. I could hardly fathom it, that at the end of a long life the physical evidence for it should be so inadequate to its depth and breadth. I felt I should be able to open the book of my mother's life and glimpse multiple interiors in three dimensions, vast tracts of earth and sea traversed, eras, skies, a thousand roads. Instead there were a few dishes and wine glasses, some laundry, shampoos and creams I didn't know whether to use or discard.

Hanging from the doorknob of my mother's walk-in closet was an ochre-coloured canvas beach bag I had given her. I'd got it my first year in Nairobi, when I was on safari, and along the bottom were tiny animals – giraffes and zebras and elephants and lions parading in a line, all the outlandish animals God had made and in which my mother took such delight. I had a vague recollection of much fuss having been made over the bag. My mother was good at that sort of thing, expressing gratitude for even the humblest of gifts, and it was for the memory of that, that particular strain of generosity, that I took the bag and placed it on her bed, along with a few other items, random to the eyes of anyone but me, that I would bring with me when I left.

In the spare bedroom, in a bag already packed, were my letters to her – one thing she *had* saved. They had petered out in the early 2000s, when she got email, but in the last years of her life, every time I visited her, she took me into the walk-in closet and showed me where all her papers were and which box contained my letters. She said she wanted me to have them when she was gone. She made me promise not to throw them out. It was a strange thing to contemplate, coming back into possession of the thousand thoughts I had entrusted to her. I used to wonder if, when she died, I would keep my promise. But I have, partly out of superstition and partly because one of the things I learned about my mother over the years was that she was usually right, and for reasons I often did not understand until long after the fact.

There were lots of letters from the early days with Eddie, from our marriage, and from the end of our marriage, which had caused my mother much sadness. She had a way of intimating that I had been ungrateful – not just to Eddie, whom she adored, but to the gods – and was prone to reminding me, in so many words, that men like Eddie didn't grow on trees. I never told her what happened at the end, or why I left him. I deflected her questions until she stopped asking. She never knew that Cauley existed. I thought that at least I could spare her the sordid details, but it was also true that I couldn't have borne her disappointment with me.

There was a lot I did tell her, though. Re-reading the

letters, I was surprised by just how much. There was something touchingly naïve about how honest I'd once been with her, all the fears and plans and daily routines I'd shared, an openness that in later years contracted into circumspection, partly to protect her but also because with age I'd grown calculating about how I wanted her to think of me. And then there was that tone – common to letters generally, I think – of a rather cumbersome care, all the laboured-over details, the logistics and practicalities, the airport meeting points and copied-out train times, the elaborate directions. There was a weight to it all then, in the time before electronic communication, a concreteness. In the time that passed between one dispatch and the next, I imagine a tremendous faith hanging in the air between us, and what astonishes me still is the trust we placed in the other's continued, unwitnessed existence.

During those days in my mother's condo, I thought often of Eddie. I wondered if I should tell him of her death. I wondered how much time need pass after a divorce before the sharing of such news goes from being a courtesy to being inappropriate or intrusive. There had been such affection between Eddie and my mother, and I used to feel, after we split, that I had deprived them of each other. We had not taken that trip in the autumn that he'd suggested, we hadn't driven my mother and Stan to the Keys. I tried to remember the last time Eddie and I had been in Florida together. I recalled the three of us – I don't know where Stan was that day – going to a nature reserve, where we rode bikes along a canal on a path as smooth as marble. The day was clear and bright and not too hot, it was winter, and alligators lolled fatly on the banks. To me they were creatures of the most obvious menace, but they brought out a strange whimsy in my mother, who was, as she might've said herself, *tickled* by the sight of them. I was aware that I was flanked by the two people who mattered most to me in the world and I felt, as I always do at such rare moments of contentment, shy and a little furtive in the face of my good luck, as though, if it were noticed, it might be taken from me.

I let myself in the front door and inhale the air of the entry-way, certain, now that I am moving out, that I can smell the sea again. On the landing are my half-packed cases and the boxes I had shipped from Nairobi. I am leaving the house in two days. I have taken an apartment just down the sea road in Dún Laoghaire, a place that would fit inside the kitchen of this house. I could've afforded more space if I'd gone else-where in the city, but I've grown attached to the view. From the fourth-floor window of my new apartment, I'll be able to see the harbour, the tides moving in and out, the lights along the shore at Howth slithering like a whip into the sea.

I wonder sometimes what my mother saw at the end, and whether it frightened her. What I imagine is her walking calmly and with resolve into the sea. This isn't altogether disconcerting. My mother adored the sea. Every time I vis-ited we would go on a boat ride, and she and Stan would lean on the rail, side by side, like children, pointing out the dolphins or the pelicans. They had embarked with such enthusiasm on the second act of their lives, and I am certain they felt repaid in kind – they had a habit of giving thanks for their good fortune.

I used to wonder if Eddie and I would be as lucky. I tried to picture us old. I thought he would age well: he would be one of those large, rough-hewn men, hale and rugged and still desirable. Solid as a house. I wanted to be there for that. I wanted to witness his life, to feel the heft of him beside me for the rest of our days. But then a kind of vertigo stole over me, like when you're standing at a height and looking out and down, thinking, *I could do it, I could just jump*, the call of the void, and all the life and death that is in your power.

This morning I went to our old house, Eddie's and mine. I left Dublin after breakfast and by noon was parked on the laneway running parallel to the mountain. I sat there eyeing the house like someone who'd been hired to tail whoever lived there. The new owners were already *in situ*. There was a car in the drive, the lawn was tended, there were potted plants on a front deck that had been added. On the path running along the side of the house was a child's three-wheeler. In spite of this evidence, the house looked deserted, eerily still, as though its inhabitants had fled, abruptly, in the face of some threat. I rolled down my window and stared and stared. Nothing emanated from it, nothing arose in me. It was like being shown a photo of myself at a gathering that I couldn't recall having attended. The disparity between the richness of our days and the scratch marks they leave behind is so great it's a wonder we trust so easily in their connection.

I remembered meeting Eddie on the street that day in town shortly after I'd moved out, the shock of estrangement, which was itself an echo of intimacy. Now I could see us on the path that led to the front door, Eddie turning the key to let us in. I saw him standing in the kitchen, gazing out the back window the way he used to, the mountain pitiless and beautiful against every kind of sky. I thought of Eddie, and I felt self-conscious, and uneasy, and full of remorse, but there was also something tender, a kind of compassion for whoever it was we'd once believed ourselves to be. I thought of our last summer together, how there are things we're unable to say even to ourselves, things we can only enact, as though we cannot believe they are what we really want until they become the only alternative we've left ourselves.

I went to Kevin's house, too. I had trouble finding it. I had held in my memory something like a child's drawing of the peninsula – the curve of shoreline, a single laneway, the house perched proud and cheerful. But I found myself driving around on a web of roads that felt unfamiliar, and visibility was bad; a heavy rain had turned the landscape blurred and viscous. Eventually, after many U-turns and much doubling back, I found the road. The skies cleared. In the sudden yellow sunshine, the house sprung up before me.

I hadn't told Kevin I was coming. I didn't have a number for him. But country people are strange. You show up at their door after a long absence and they greet you as though your arrival were the very thing they'd been expecting. Kevin had the front door open before I was even out of the car. He must've seen me passing slowly and then reversing. We greeted each other shyly. We had never been close, but we had once colluded in something ruinous, and I felt with him the sort of intimacy I might feel with a doctor who'd given me news of a terrible illness.

He'd grown skinny. The baby fat, what we all had back then and would never have thought of as such, was gone. His hair was grey and thinning. He led me into the sitting room, which was no longer catastrophic but looked simply like the home of a middle-aged bachelor, lived in, but thinly, as though it would take only an hour's labour to remove all trace of him.

He asked me how I'd been. I wasn't sure where to begin, or what to leave out or include. I said that I was living in Dublin, that I was on a career break, sort of, that I'd been working abroad. I told him that my mother had died. He said that his mother had also died, and that his father was in a nursing home in town. He told me he'd had a lot of offers on his little house during the boom and had been sorely tempted but was glad he hadn't sold. He'd had to quit the building sites, he said. He had injured his shoulder in an accident and couldn't do heavy work.

I pretended to look around the sitting room, then glanced over my shoulder towards the spare bedroom, which was behind me. 'Would you mind?'

'Work away,' he said, as though it were the most natural thing in the world, my turning up out of the blue like that to poke around his spare bedroom.

If ever there was a case of a person going back and finding the room, the house, the yard, larger than remembered, I have not heard of it. The bedroom was as tiny as a jail cell. I recognized the wardrobe: it was the same one against which Kevin had propped those huge triangles of glass. Now there were two bicycle tyres leaning on it, and a pump lying on the floor. Against the wall to the right of the door was the bed. I was tired, and I looked longingly at it, the way you do beds in furniture shops. And then I sat and stared straight ahead of me to where a window should've been. I recalled, as clearly as I do any of the scenes from that house, Cauley and me lying on the rumpled sheets and the sun streaming in through the large picture window opposite that looked out over the bedraggled front lawn, beyond which we could see, in the distance, the mountain looming behind my own house. But in reality, there was only a small sash window to the right, facing on to the gravel drive and a bank of trees that separated Kevin's property from the neighbour's.

I heard Kevin behind me.

'Y'all right?' he said. I got up quickly, and we scanned the room, as though for clues.

I thought of asking him to leave me alone for a few more minutes, so I could get my fill of whatever it was I'd come for – forgiveness or consolation or a rush of youth.

'I'm fine,' I said, and we turned and shuffled out.

He invited me to stay for lunch. In the kitchen, he opened the fridge, which was clean, if mostly empty, and took out a bottle of mineral water. The floors were swept, I noticed. The stovetop was scrubbed, the kitchen chairs stood uniformly at the table.

'The place looks good,' I said.

'And me?' Kevin said. 'Do I look good?'

I turned to him. He busied himself finding a bottle opener for the water.

'You do, actually.'

He pried the cap off and said, 'I should hope so.'

He told me that by the end of that summer he was having trouble remembering the most familiar things: the name of the woman in the local shop, the meaning of items he'd written on a grocery list, his mother's phone number. 'It was like

I had fucking Alzheimer's,' he said. So someone had dragged him to the hospital, and he dried out for two weeks with Librium and then did ninety meetings in ninety days. After the first one, in a community centre up on John Street, about a dozen people had come up to him and shook his hand and said, 'We thought you'd never get here,' as though he were delivering supplies to some desperate outpost.

He got a head of lettuce and a cucumber from the fridge and then went out back to where he'd planted a small garden, a raised bed in a plot of trimmed grass I didn't remember from before – the image I'd retained was of the world stopping at the edge of Kevin's patio wall. He picked scallions and dug up carrots and tossed everything together, then got two chipped plates out of the cupboard and some unmatched cutlery, and a few slices of brown bread. We brought the whole lot outside and set it on a table made of a flat slab of rock. There were short stools of cracked vinyl that must've come from a pub, and we perched on them like little old ladies on a Sunday afternoon, sipping our fizzy water and eating our salad.

'Do you ever hear from him?' I asked.

'He's in London.'

I knew that much. I saw it on the internet. He runs a small theatre company there. His wife is a set designer.

'He went a bit off the rails, you know.'

I hadn't known, but it was easy to imagine. Cauley was wired, on a collision course with something – even I could see it, as heedless as I was then, all the energy he didn't yet know how to harness.

'But he pulled it together. He's married, he's got two boys. He came out to the house a few months ago.'

'Really?' It shouldn't have surprised me that Cauley still visited: he and Kevin had been friends since childhood. But I was startled to think of him here so recently.

Kevin poured what was left of the water into our glasses, then drained his. A bird hopped brightly on the wall. The sun was shining. It was steamy then, after the rain, like we were in the tropics. A hundred metres down the road was the wide sandy beach. I envied him, in a way. A house of his own, the sea on his doorstep. Knowing what his life consisted of, and where it was rooted. A life of limits isn't necessarily easier, but there is something clarifying in it, and beauty makes up for a lot.

It was late afternoon when I left Kevin, heading back to town along the sea road. Crossing the bridge, I could see the hostel where I had lived that first summer. To the left, the low, drab skyline of Stephen Street, and to the right the docks, where Eddie's showroom and flat had been. Then I was back on the relief road, which had finally been built, carved right through the town's centre, houses bulldozed to make way. High walls of forbidding grey stone had been erected either side of it, so that I felt I was driving past a prison, or out of one.

The house creaks and ticks, as though light-footed creatures are living their little lives all around me. I sit down at the kitchen table and make a list for tomorrow. Harry is coming for brunch. He said we're going to have a reverse housewarming. I asked him what that meant, and he said that it was when, instead of imprinting yourself upon a new place through objects, you think about what the place you're leaving has given you, the intangible things, and how you'll bring those with you to the next life. 'By which I mean,' he said, 'the next place you live.'

I nodded. It sounded interesting. 'Is that a ritual?' I asked. 'Where do they do this?'

He shrugged, smiling. 'I made it up.'

I picture Harry in the kitchen here, conjuring on my behalf. I remember what he said once about how everywhere you leave stays with you. In a satchel on the table in front of me, in a wallet-sized folder that holds nothing else, is a photo of my mother. It is my favourite of the dozens I've held on to. She is four years old, and the look of bliss on her face as she stands ankle-deep in the Pacific is more than I know what to do with. Her head is tilted up and her eyes are closed, as though she has heard a whisper from on high. I look at that child and I hold her in the kind of awe in which my mother once held me. I feel my mother less acutely than I did even one week ago. But what I lose in intensity I seem to gain in diffuseness: I feel her everywhere. I think of her belongings, the few I saved. From where I'm sitting I can see them, in a box on the landing, awaiting transport to the next life.

# Acknowledgements

Thanks to the Arts Council of Ireland for their ongoing and generous support. Thank you to Brendan Barrington, Lucy Luck, Mary Costello, Una Mannion, Adam, Ciarán, and the Searson family of Monkstown.

This novel grew out of a short story, 'City of Glass', which appeared in *Town & Country: New Irish Short Stories*. Thanks to Kevin Barry, who edited that anthology.

The lines 'What does it mean,' he asks, 'when people say, "She's out of her misery"? Why the present tense? Who's this *she* we're speaking of?' (p. 37) are based on lines from Roland Barthes' *Mourning Diary*: 'In the sentence "She's no longer suffering," to what, to whom does "she" refer? What does that present tense mean?'

# He just wanted a decent book to read ...

Not too much to ask, is it? It was in 1935 when Allen Lane, Managing Director of Bodley Head Publishers, stood on a platform at Exeter railway station looking for something good to read on his journey back to London. His choice was limited to popular magazines and poor-quality paperbacks – the same choice faced every day by the vast majority of readers, few of whom could afford hardbacks. Lane's disappointment and subsequent anger at the range of books generally available led him to found a company – and change the world.

*'We believed in the existence in this country of a vast reading public for intelligent books at a low price, and staked everything on it'*
**Sir Allen Lane, 1902–1970, founder of Penguin Books**

The quality paperback had arrived – and not just in bookshops. Lane was adamant that his Penguins should appear in chain stores and tobacconists, and should cost no more than a packet of cigarettes.

Reading habits (and cigarette prices) have changed since 1935, but Penguin still believes in publishing the best books for everybody to enjoy. We still believe that good design costs no more than bad design, and we still believe that quality books published passionately and responsibly make the world a better place.

So wherever you see the little bird – whether it's on a piece of prize-winning literary fiction or a celebrity autobiography, political tour de force or historical masterpiece, a serial-killer thriller, reference book, world classic or a piece of pure escapism – you can bet that it represents the very best that the genre has to offer.

**Whatever you like to read – trust Penguin.**